Magic and the Terror at Loch Ness

Gale Gene

Brilliant Books Literary
137 Forest Park Lane Thomasville
North Carolina 27360 USA

Dedicated to:
My awesome children,
Our beautiful Wiley,
Faith and
Encouragement

Hebrews 13:2
Be not forgetful to entertain strangers; for thereby
some have entertained angels unawares.

CONTENTS

ATLANTIC OCEAN
NORTH SEA
SKYE
NORTHERN HIGHLANDS
INVERNESS
LOCH NESS
SCOTLAND
EDINBURGH
IRELAND
NORTHERN IRELAND
NORTH SEA

◆ ◆ ◆ ◆ ◆ ◆

CHAPTER ONE
SURPRISE

It is a typical summer morning in Southern California… Los Angeles, to be exact. The fog is a thick blanket hiding the sun. It is what is commonly known in this region as 'June gloom'. The morning starts out gloomy, and, finally about noon, the blazing sun peeks through the fog bank, eventually chasing the fog completely away to expose royal blue skies. There is always a brownish haze that clusters around the inland horizon or the coastal horizon, depending upon which way the wind blew the day before…that's *smog.* Once the sun is out, the beach buzz escalates. Coastal junkies of Southern California curse the 'June gloom' as it puts a damper on their sun worshipping, skin cancer or not. They just don't care. You know…'That will never happen to me' mentality.

The neighborhood is a beachcombing paradise: bicycles and bikinis, board shorts and surfboards and boogie boards loaded with supplies for the day. Beach-goers drag boogie boards down the sidewalks toward the beach along narrow streets packed with quaint, expensive homes. Eventually, this routine will bring these impatient water babies through the scorching, coarse sand, ending the quest at the cool, green-blue ocean and the crashing surf. Sun worshipers compete for parking spaces, while traffic slows to accommodate the beach scene. The smell of sunscreen and moist, salty air hangs in the gentle morning breeze. This particular area of Venice Beach flaunts different styles of homes dating back to 1912. The oldest ones have been restored. There are Craftsman style homes made with wood and large porches, Spanish style homes with tiled roofs, and little wooden bungalows that resemble typical beach houses from the

1920's. Every house is different. There are a few 1970's condos thrown in to the mix. It is an eclectic mix of style and neighbors. Trees and plants surround the homes nurtured by the seashore mist.

On this especially quiet, overcast, early dawn…before the beach paradise awakens…there is a deafening crackle and the fog breaks apart… revealing a blinding, bright, neon yellow light resembling a lightning bolt. The dawn air becomes still. The bolt fades and standing in the middle of the neighborhood street, as plain as day, is a man wearing a satiny robe the color and brightness of the lightning bolt. His hair is like a flaming, bright star. He has huge, transparent silver wings fluttering around him. This brilliantly lit man is holding an awkward, shimmering object. The object floats to the ground. It appears to be a container of a sort. Out hop five fluffy, twinkling, golden-retriever puppies. These gold fur balls with sparkly eyes and fur are sniffing the misty air. The brilliant man scoops up the puppies in a flash…as another bright, neon yellow bolt crackles in the sky, and they are gone.

Sitting on its tail in the middle of the street is one of the golden puppies. The fluffy, fur ball sits sniffing the salty, morning air. The puppy heads towards one of the larger, old bungalow houses; The house is painted forest green with white trim and a white picket fence surrounds it. A boy's fire engine red, Schwinn beach cruiser, long black skateboard and a worn boogie board decorate the front yard and porch. Heading around the back, the golden puppy prances, as if it knows where it's going. Around the back of the house, it stops, sniffs the air and stares at the window directly above it on the second floor.

Down it flops on the grass, resting its chin on its paws as if waiting for something.

◆ ◆ ◆ ◆ ◆ ◆ ◆

CHAPTER TWO
THE GANG

My album is starting to fall apart after years of flipping through it. The album is such a random book of memories. My mom started it, and I just keep adding to it. My baby picture and birth certificate are on the first page. God really gave my mom and dad a boy who fits his name, Paul Wonder. You see… I wonder a lot about everything, and always go investigating to discover what I am wondering about. I seem to always be seeking adventure and finding it, along with uncanny mysteries and trouble. The cool thing about my adventures is my dog, *Magic*… She always seems to be in the middle of my adventures, making them happen. I have lots of pictures of her. She IS like *Magic*.

I don't have a regular type family, so I need to explain about our rather odd situation, especially *Magic*. Everyone I'll mention plays an important part in my life and adventures.

I live with my dad, my aunt, my grandma and my dog, *Magic*, in Venice Beach, which is in Santa Monica, California. It is close to Hollywood, which we visit quite often. Hollywood is a very populated area with all kinds of action, especially movie stars.

We like to drive up through Beverly Hills and check out the mansions. It is kinda in the heart of Los Angeles. My mom, Rebekah, died of cancer when I was seven. She was my best friend and hero. I know that sounds cornball, but it's true. She was my hero because she could do anything to make everything right. I knew I could always count on her to be with me and help me with anything.

One time I got really sick with chicken pox. My lungs got infected, because I have infectious asthma. That means, when I get sick, my asthma flares up, and then I get really sick. She waited on me hand and foot. I never felt lonely or sad, because she bought me a new Lego set of a pirate ship, and made good things to eat, and sat with me while we watched movies and read together.

My mom never seemed a bit sick, but I guess it was a surprise cancer. All of a sudden, she was gone. Things really changed when she died, because it was like I had no parent, as my dad wasn't around much because of his job. I can't understand why God took her from me, but my dad said that I would see her in heaven. Now I am thirteen, and I still miss her. I keep pictures of her and me in my room, so I will never forget what she looked like. It is weird how the memory of the way someone looks might fade, but the feelings I had for her have never stopped. My dad says she is always with me, as long as I never forget about her and the way she was.

My dad's name is Noah, and he is a filmmaker. He travels around to different countries and films movies about nature, travel and adventures. He was not home much when my mom was still with us, but since she left, we have become closer. I think he feels guilty. He probably realizes that he missed out on our lives. He goes to places like Italy, Greece, England and Africa. Sometimes I get to go, if I am on a break from school. He always says that when I get older, I can go with him and do my studies on the road. My dad is a small, hyper man. Everyone says I look like him. He has red hair and so do I. I guess I look like him, but I think I will be taller, because I am only thirteen and I can already look him directly in the eyes. We have the same smile with big teeth. We both love action and movies, and I even get to help him film sometimes. My favorite thing is camping, hiking and sailing with my dad, because we fish and talk and play with *Magic*. Since Mom has been gone, we do these things together more often. His filming takes us places, so we can do these things while he films a movie. It's cool.

Aunt Rue, as I call her, came to live with us after my mom left. Everyone else calls her Ruthie. She is a detective and works for the Los Angeles Police Department. The hours she works are really strange, and she is always on call, which means she is always thinking like a detective.

My dad thinks it is sad that she spends most of her life with criminals. I think her job is exciting, but I am an adventure seeker, so that kind of existence appeals to me. Aunt Rue is a tiny person, which is kinda weird for a police detective. My dad and she look alike, because of the red hair. Red hair is like that. Either everyone in the family has it, or it pops up after a few generations as a shocking surprise. My aunt moved in with us after my mom left, because she knew someone needed to help Dad raise me. Aunt Rue is much younger than my dad. She is really funny and has lots of bizarre stories, especially when she works undercover. It is like a constant adventure when she is around. She likes to include Dad and me in her life as much as possible, because she doesn't date much, as she thinks most men are boring. Everything seems boring to her, since her job is so unpredictable.

The last, but not least, relative that I need to tell you about is my grandma. Her name is Bernice, but everyone calls her 'Bernie'… except me. I call her Grandma. Her main focus, besides church and me, is food. She prepares food and serves it at parties. It is called a catering business. She concocts tasty food and plenty of it. Two of her good friends from church help her with the business, so they hang around a lot. They love to have parties and go to parties, so this is the perfect business for them. Their specialties are parties in Hollywood and theme marriages. Theme marriages are when people get married, and they pick a theme for their wedding. I notice a lot of wedding themes are Italian or European. Lately, the popular theme has been the 1920's. It is strange, but people start acting crazy when they plan weddings. My grandma and her friends prepare the food that goes with the theme of the celebration they are catering. Then they deliver the food, set it up and serve it.

My dad is happy about the catering business. He doesn't like to cook. My Aunt Rue works odd hours, so she doesn't cook. My friends and everyone who knows us are all thankful for my grandma's obsession with food. I think my grandma is young for a grandma, because she is really pretty and active. She is taller than my dad, aunt and I. I hope I got her genes, so I will be tall. She doesn't have red hair though. It's long and brown/gray and curly. She wears it up a lot. She says she's too old to wear it down but doesn't want short hair. Grandma moved in with us after my mom left. I guess everyone felt like they wanted to help fill the hole my mom left in our hearts. People are strange that way, because no one could ever fill her special section in my heart. I don't know about my dad. He never said much about her dying. I know he misses her, though, because he always talks about her and has never gone out on a date. My mom was the only child, and her parents were killed in a freak boating accident, so I never really have much contact with my mom's other relatives. I am glad dad has a mom and a sister around.

Our house is a meeting place for all good friends, it seems. My grandma always opens our house to any of our friends who need a place to go. I like being able to invite friends over when I want to spend more time with them. Grandma has her community group meeting from church every Wednesday night at our house. Groups of people, most of them single and older, come to our house to study the Bible and eat good food that my grandma prepares. They all love that she hosts the Bible study, because there is always good food. I am not expected to participate in the grown ups meeting… thankfully. I have my Bible study at school everyday, because I go to a Christian school in our neighborhood.

I need to tell you about one member of our family, which we could not live without, at least in my opinion.

She needs a chapter to herself…It is quite a story…

◆ ◆ ◆ ◆ ◆ ◆

CHAPTER THREE
MAGIC

Our house is in constant action…but I like that. We all have fun and help each other. My dog, **Magic**, is the most important member of our family. She is really unique because of her size and her hair and her eyes. **Magic** is a huge golden retriever with tons of hair that, **I** think, actually sparkles like gold crystals in the sunlight, if the sun catches her fur just right. Her hair keeps growing and we have to keep cutting it. Her head is like the size of a St. Bernard. You know the dog in the movie Beethoven? ***Magic's eyes sometimes twinkle with a yellow glow when they are in the sunlight.***

My dad says I'm crazy, and my Aunt Rue rolls her eyes, and my grandma tells my dad to let me have an imagination…but **Magic** really does sparkle sometimes. She looks so much like the golden retriever my mom used to have, before I was born. They could be sisters. My mom's dog was Cleo. I know my mom would have loved **Magic** like we do. Mom had tons of pictures of Cleo like I have of **Magic**. She had a whole album of pictures from when Cleo was a puppy until she got old. I guess we both love dogs.

The first time I noticed **Magic's** eyes sparkling like stars was when a car almost hit me. She was still a puppy. My best friends, Jacob and Micah and I were playing a game called "Ditch em"…like hide and seek. I was running to get to home base, my front porch, and I didn't even look to check for cars. I went bounding across the street. It was a very narrow street with little traffic. Surprisingly, a little red sports car was coming down the street on my right. Miraculously, I jumped over the hood of the car to land safely on the other side.

Magic was watching the whole thing sitting on the curb, near the porch I was trying to reach. As I was in the air...flabbergasted at my ability to jump that high and far... I looked at *Magic*, who was directly in my path. Her eyes were sparkling like neon yellow stars. I landed right next to her on my feet but had to run a few steps from the momentum of my jump. The guy in the car stopped a few feet up the road, lifted himself up in his seat, as he looked at me, and shook his head and fist at me. We were worried that he was going to come and yell at us.

After he drove on, I went to *Magic* and knelt down in front of her to look at her eyes. They had lost that neon yellow star look, but were shimmering slightly yellow, as they sometimes do in the sun. She licked my face and stood up and wagged her tail. Jacob and Micah were standing on the porch with their mouths open in amazement after seeing me jump over the car.

"How did you do that?" Jacob exclaimed.

Micah shouted, "That was awesome!"

I stood up and looked back at the street, shook my head and marveled, "That was a miracle. I must have an angel watching over me." I exclaimed.

Micah replied, "Where can I get an angel like that?" They both came towards me, and we started shoving each other around playfully while *Magic* danced. It was definitely a magical moment. I didn't tell my friends about *Magic*'s eyes...because I was beginning to wonder if I had imagined it.

Magic has always been our family's mystery. It is really weird the way we found her. It all started before my tenth birthday...

I kept bugging my dad for a puppy claiming I was lonely. I pleaded with him, "Dad, please let me get a puppy. I promise I will do everything I can do for it. I'll feed it, give it a bath, brush it and walk it." I kept trying to assure him that I would do all the work.

He always just said, "How could you be lonely with all the action in this house? I know who will get stuck picking up the dog poop... me."

He also kept saying, "What about when we go on our trips? What will we do with it then?"

I kept insisting, "Dad, we could take the dog with us. It could help us with all our adventures. Think of the responsibility it would teach me."

Dad looked at me seriously, shook his head and chuckled.

For some reason my dad was being really stubborn about the dog. Aunt Rue wanted one too. She thought we could use a watchdog. Grandma was worried a dog might steal food. I thought everyone would adjust to a dog. I always thought that every kid needed a dog.

I dropped the subject, because I didn't want my dad to get angry. I figured that I would just wait a week or two and maybe bring it up right before my birthday next month. Since my birthday was in June, I figured it would be a good time to get a puppy because I would be off for the summer. Dad was usually pretty laid back about stuff, but this dog idea was a real contention between us.

About three weeks later, at the beginning of June, a really weird thing happened. It was a Saturday morning, and I was sleeping in. Since June is always gloomy, I didn't care if I slept late on Saturdays. I woke up because I was cold and noticed my window was open. I usually sleep with it closed, except when it is really hot. I started to crawl out of bed to shut it, wanting to sleep longer. My foot hit something solid on my bed. I looked toward the bottom of my bed, and I couldn't believe what I saw. There, at the bottom of my bed, curled into a ball, was a glimmering, golden, fluffy puppy...sound asleep. I poked at it, thinking it was a stuffed animal that my dad put there to tease me with, because it didn't look like a real dog... Dad did stuff like that sometimes.

The puppy flinched when I poked it. I got closer to have a better look, and up popped its head. We were nose to nose. Its eyes were **literally** shimmering, neon yellow. That was really weird. This dog had sparkling eyes. *My birthday*, I thought... *Dad got it for my birthday!* I scooped up the fur ball into my arms, scurried out of my room, through the hall and down the stairs. I raced through the house to the kitchen at the back of the house, and burst in yelling, "Dad, Dad, thanks, thanks! You really surprised me this time! I thought you were serious about no puppy! It's the greatest present ever!"

Dad had just poured himself a cup of coffee and stood by the window, which faced out into our backyard. He had a very weird expression on his face as he exclaimed, "Where did you get that puppy?"

I thought that he must be joking, but he looked so serious. *Maybe my Aunt Rue got it for me,* I decided silently.

I replied hesitantly… "Didn't you get it for me?"

Dad set his coffee down on the breakfast table and came toward me with a curious look on his face. "I did not get you a puppy. What kind of trick is this? You know my decision about having a dog around."

I felt my heart racing, and I stammered and responded defensively, "Uh… Uh…it was sleeping at the foot of my bed when I woke a few minutes ago. Honest. I would never get a dog by myself after you told me 'No'. Really!"

My Aunt Rue and Grandma entered the kitchen, stopped and smiled when they saw me holding the puppy. They both exclaimed at the same time, "A golden puppy!"

My aunt said to my dad, "Oh, you old softy. I knew you'd give in to him about the puppy. It looks like Rebekah's puppy Cleo."

Dad just stood there looking confused.

Grandma said, "Boy, are we gonna have our hands full with that fur ball. Look at the size of its feet. It's gonna be a big one."

Check out its fur." I exclaimed as she came closer. "It has a little sparkle to it."

"Wait just a minute here. What is going on? Did I miss something? Where the heck did this puppy come from?" Dad looked at his mom and sister and said, "Was this one of your ideas?"

"What?" Aunt Rue and Grandma said at the same time. They looked at each other confused.

"What do you mean?" exclaimed Grandma.

"Didn't you get the puppy for Paul?" Aunt Rue questioned Dad.

"No, I didn't. I told all of you we were not getting a puppy," Dad insisted. "Paul, you have some explaining to do."

All eyes were on me. I looked down at the golden fur ball, and it began to lick my face. I laughed and said "Come on Dad, you must have bought the puppy. How else could it be here? I didn't get it. Aunt Rue and Grandma didn't get it. So how could it just show up on my bed? I got up to close my window, and…ah, wait a minute. Did you open my window after I went to bed last night dad?"

"No," replied Dad.

"Your window was open this morning? You didn't open it?" Aunt Rue questioned, always on the alert for unsafe situations.

"No." I insisted as the puppy continued to lick my face and wiggled to get loose. I held it up and looked at its tummy. "It's a girl puppy," I exclaimed as I set her on the floor. She started sniffing around, and lumbered over to my dad and put her front paws up on his legs, tail wagging, tongue hanging out as if she was smiling at him. He bent down and scooped her up to get a closer look, and practically got a bath from the tongue licking.

"How do you suppose she got into our house?" I asked.

Dad looked around the puppy's neck for a tag or something that might indicate where she was from. Then my dad took off quickly from the kitchen, through the house, up the stairs and down the hall to my room. We all followed wondering what Dad was up to. When he got to my room, he walked directly to the window and looked out. The screen was missing. My dad turned and looked at us with a confused look.

"How could this puppy find her way up here, open the window and come in?" he questioned. He looked down at the puppy and then at us… "She must be *Magic*. That is the only explanation."

We kept the puppy. We named her *Magic.*

◆ ◆ ◆ ◆ ◆ ◆

CHAPTER FOUR
ON THE ROAD AGAIN

The summer is zipping by while Jacob, Micah and I hang at the beach most of the time. They are my two best friends I've known since second grade. We all met at church in our youth group. We hang out and look for mysterious adventures…when we finish with homework and chores and church, of course. When I complain about my chores, my dad always says, "We all have to earn our keep," whatever that means. I guess it means that we all have to contribute to our home, if we want to eat.

My one friend, Jacob, is older than me by a year. He's fourteen. My other friend, Micah, is my age. Micah and I are about the same size. Jacob is a little shorter and heavier. We have been friends since we were seven. We are inseparable, even though we are basically different. Micah is hyperactive, noisy and really annoying. Jacob is also hyper, funny and even louder and more annoying than Micah. I am pretty hyper but a little more laid back than Jacob and Micah. Jacob always wants to go body surfing or surfing, rain or shine, big waves or no waves. Micah always has mischievous ideas that usually get us into trouble. I have my share of ideas too, but am a little more cautious, because my aunt Rue gets really mad, because …what we do is usually borderline illegal.

What I mean by illegal is, one time, we decided to put on our fatigues (my grandma found them at a garage sale from ex-marines), take our paintball guns and ammo, sneak through all the neighbor's yards and have paintball fights. Evidently, doing that is not only dangerous but also illegal…scolded my Aunt Rue. That was the last time we tried that.

Jacob, Micah and I are never at a loss for fun, or, as my dad calls it, trouble seeking. My aunt and grandma really have their hands full with us, since we always hang out at my house. Jacob lives with his mom and his grandparents. His grandpa is a retired navy captain, so he runs a tight ship at Jacob's house. Micah lives in an apartment with his mom and her boyfriend, so Micah has a lot of responsibilities. He has to get straight 'A's' in school, or his mom will have a fit. He has to help around the house a lot, so he likes to stay at my house. Everyone always wants to stay a my house.

We meet our friends from school at the beach every day in the summer and spend the days body surfing and licking our wounds, after our battles with the ocean floor. The blanket of coarse sand and pebbles, with an occasional rock being ground into our knees, palms and cheeks can be ravaging. Spinning in the surf also has its drawbacks…but when you catch that perfect wave…the thrill of speeding above the ocean floor, scanning the beach and all the swimmers below, is worth every scrape, mouthful of water and feeling of doom. A perfect ending to the quest of the perfect wave is my grandma's food, which is always waiting for us when we return to my house, bedraggled from the surf and sun.

It is a stifling hot day in August, as we walk home exhausted in anticipation of what feast will be awaiting us.

"Grandma was working on a Mexican feast when we left this morning," I volunteer to Jacob and Micah on the way home. I didn't want to tell them this morning, as they would have wanted to come home sooner.

"Now you tell us." Micah responds.

"Hey Grandma," I call as we open the screen on the back door.

"Did you wash the sand off?" She never fails to warn us. "Don't let *Magic* out. She will get all sandy jumping around and bring it in with her."

For obvious reasons *Magic*, couldn't come to the beach with us. Sometimes I take her down at night or early morning for a run.

"We're doing that now. What's to eat? It smells amazing." I call, as Jacob and Micah are already thoroughly involved in a water fight with the spray nozzle.

"Cut it out. You'll get everything wet, and Grandma will have to clean everything up, or I will!" I exclaim. I never want to wreck a good thing, and coming home to Grandma's feast is definitely a good thing.

"You are in luck today. Phoebe, Mary (grandma's two friends that help her with the catering business) and I have been cooking all day for a Mexican fiesta-wedding feast. There are tacos, enchiladas, rice, empanadas, flan and other tidbits. Are you cleaned off?" Grandma asks, as she looks us over with her usual inspection.

"Yeah…and hungry!" Jacob, Micah and I chime in together. We hustle to the long, wooden, farm style kitchen table. I love the table, because we can fit twelve people around it easily. It is thick and wide and has really sturdy chairs, so we don't have to be so careful. We can sit around it and play board games without being cramped, which is always our favorite summer evening activity. I guess my dad knew what he was doing when he bought it. No frills or fancy furniture in our house. There are too many people coming through all the time, most of them being my friends. Guys are not that easy on things. It is not that we don't care. It is just we don't always pay attention to what we're doing.

Grandma hands us a plate and tell us to have at it. The feast is spread around the kitchen counters and on half of the table. The smell is amazing. My favorite is enchiladas… Cheese, chicken, or beef…it doesn't matter. I love them all. My Grandma makes the best Mexican rice and homemade refried beans too. There are flour tortillas, corn tortillas, fresh salsa, and guacamole. We are in for a treat!

"Hey gang, what's going on? What a smell. I could smell it on the driveway out front. Boy, do I love your job, Mom!" Dad exclaims as he bounds in the door and gives Grandma a hug. He is very close with his mom because she raised him and Aunt Rue by herself, so they all took care of each other.

"It is a Mexican feast today Dad. How come you're home early?" I ask.

"Well…we are going to be 'On the Road Again'." Dad replies.

"What? We? Explain!" I excitedly reply as I am shoving forkfuls of enchiladas and beans in my mouth. Jacob and Micah are silent as they shovel in the banquet before them.

"How do you feel about Scotland?" Dad responds as he grabs his plate and starts filling it up.

"Scotland!" I exclaim as my fork stops halfway to my mouth with the next morsel. "You mean the Loch Ness monster place?"

"That's the place." Dad grins.

"What do you mean? Do I get to go? What is your job there? When do we go? How long are we gonna be there?" I question in a flurry.

"Whoa, hold your horses; One question at a time, please. I am overwhelmed by all this food…trying to get it in my mouth as soon as possible," Dad exclaims, "Give me a minute to get settled here."

"How can you be so calm?" I question as I jump up from my seat and scoot around the table to where my dad has parked himself, taco in hand. Jacob and Micah laugh and chatter between mouthfuls as they watch the scene unfurl. They're always excited about my dad's trips, especially when I am involved. They're always hoping to go along sometime. My dad always promises that they can go when they are older.

"Well, the details have not been ironed out yet, but it looks like it is going to happen. Everything should be scheduled and reservations made in a week or so. The film is going to be a vacation travel series on the attractions in the United Kingdom. Since the economy is slow, people are not traveling there as much, and tourism is suffering. There are some representatives from Vacations.com who contacted us to go to the United Kingdom and film the sights in Ireland, England and Scotland and publicize the great vacation sites that are offered there. My crew and I were chosen to take the Scotland scene. I am happy about that, since I haven't been there before. I thought this would be a great opportunity to include you and maybe even Aunt Ruthie to go with me. What do you think?" Dad asks.

"Are you kidding? That is awesome!" I exclaim. "Do you think we will see the Lock Ness monster?"

"Oh yeah, I am sure of that," Dad chuckles. "You know that is just a legend. No one has ever really seen a monster. There have been sightings of a large tail and disturbance in the water, but after all these years, no one has ever been able to come up with anything. But we will be filming by the ruins of the Urquhart Castle positioned on the lake where the monster supposedly lives. The present ruins date from the 13th to the 16th century. It played a huge role in the Wars of Scottish Independence in the 14th century. It was one of the largest castles in Scotland and was partially destroyed in 1692. Actually, it is one of the most visited castles in Scotland."

"How do you know all that?" I question.

"It sounds like we're in a history class," teases Micah.

"Oh, when I found out where we were going, I did some research. I like to know what to expect and what I will be filming, before I go somewhere. There is also a boat dock near the castle that takes people out on the lake. Tourists want to try and site the monster." Dad smirks and winks at me.

"All right, I know you think there is no such thing, but I bet we see something creepy there," I protest.

"I don't doubt that we will see some creepy things on this trip, since we will be hanging out at a variety of ancient ruins where there are probably many haunts lurking about," comments Dad.

"Still, you never know. So...we WILL be filming around where the monster is supposed to live!" I marveled. I had always been obsessed with Scotland and the monster. I had read several books about those who had searched for the monster. I even had a children's book that my mom used to read to me all the time about a little boy whose uncle brought him an egg from Scotland and it hatched into a monster. I need to find that book, I thought. My mom's family is from Scotland. My dad's is from Ireland.

"Yes," Dad continues. "We have to tour around several areas of Scotland. There are many attractions in Scotland that interest tourist, like the Edinburgh castle, which is in the middle of a town called Edinburgh...imagine that. A really cool thing is that there is an event happening in Edinburgh called the Fringe festival, which has all kinds of artists, plays, exhibits and street performers. The festival happens every year in August. People come from everywhere to see it. There are sword swallowers and street operas and food. It sounds like quite the festival. There is also St. Andrews golf course around this area, where many major golf tournaments are held. Inverness is a town a couple of hours north of Edinburgh in the highlands, better known to you as the mountains, where Lock Ness runs through. Lock Ness is a lake and river where 'Nessie' the monster supposedly hangs out. Lock is the Gaelic word for lake. There are several islands up near the highlands. Also, there are castles everywhere. Some of them are used in movies. I think it will be quite the medieval experience."

Micah and Jacob put down their forks and are totally awe struck by Dad's description of Scotland. "We want to go," they both chimed in together. Everyone laughs. It is perfect timing.

"I'd love to take you, but not this time." Dad replies. "You guys are not old enough to be on your own in another country. I won't have the time to watch out for you, and I'm sure Aunt Ruthie will have my head if I leave her in charge. She probably wants to enjoy the trip, if she decides to go. She could use a nice break from chasing criminals, don't you think?" Dad replies.

"Oh, we wouldn't be a problem. Really. We would stay out of the way. We could just explore while you film and Aunt Ruthie relaxes and does some sightseeing," pleads the boys.

"Where will I be relaxing?" asks Aunt Rue as she bangs in the back door.

"Scotland," Micah and Jacob blurt out excitedly again in unison.

"You guys should start your own band. Your timing is impressive. Scotland, Ruthie. What do you think? Would you like to do some relaxing in Scotland?" asks Dad.

"Not if these jokers are going to be hanging around." Aunt Rue answers. "I deal with enough drama at work, let alone on vacation, You're not thinking of turning me loose with these goofballs in Scotland, are you?"

"Hey, hey, hey...watch it now," Jacob and I respond.

"You know you love us," says Micah.

Dad replies, "No, not this trip. You would only have to deal with Paul and me. One of these days, though, I will take all you guys. It will probably be when you are 15. How does that sound?"

"Really?" We all question.

"If you can show me in the next couple of years that you are up to it, I will consider, but, right now, are you in?" Dad questions Aunt Rue.

"When is this all taking place?" Aunt Rue asks with a tinge of excitement starting to build in her voice.

I love Aunt Rue because of her excitement whenever there is a possible adventure. She and I always manage to get involved with something, even when we are going to relax. Relaxation always turns into a quest of some kind or another, and *Magic* is always at the center of it. "Do you think we might get a peak at that monster?" Aunt Rue adds. Her and I always talk and read about the infamous monster.

"Monsters, always monsters," complains Dad. "If all goes as planned, we should be on our way in a week or so. Don't you have vacation time available? I noticed you haven't taken a vacation lately."

Before Aunt Rue can answer, Grandma, who has been listening intently to the whole spiel while preparing her containers, says. "What about me? Don't I deserve a vacation? I want to go to Scotland."

We all look at Grandma, and shift our heads the other way to look at Dad to see what he will say. It is suddenly quiet. Dad finishes his mouthful of enchiladas, wipes his face with the blue and white-checkered napkin, (Grandma always had cloth napkins that matched everything in her kitchen, which had an Italian theme of blue and white checks with roosters everywhere) and retorts, "Well, if you can get away, come on along."

"Wheeeee," Grandma squeals while she throws her hands in the air. "We are going to Scotland," She sings as she dances around the kitchen hooking arms with Aunt Rue while she swings her around.

"Oh, this is going to be one for the books," groans Dad.

"Oh, we will have a blast," responds Aunt Rue.

"Of course, we have to take *Magic*," I add.

◆ ◆ ◆ ◆ ◆ ◆

Chapter Five
ALL ABOARD

Everything goes as planned, and we are scheduled to be on our way to Scotland via New York in eight days. It all happens so suddenly; I hardly have time for that anxiety I always get before a trip. You know, things like worrying about getting sick, or forgetting the most important thing, or will *Magic* be okay by herself in the cage, or will I get lost, or will we miss our plane, or not being able to sleep weeks before the trip because of all the stress involved with traveling internationally, or on and on and on. I guess I am kind of a worrier. I think I get it from my mom. Everyone says that she was always very protective of me and anxious when we traveled.

My dad always reassures me, "God is watching over us, and we must trust him to help us through life. God has a plan, and, even though we are sometimes afraid about what will happen, we need to put our trust in God." I think that this way of thinking is why my dad is always so calm about traveling or things that just happen unexpectedly, like when my mom died.

My dad and I pray together every night before bed, so God knows we want him to be in our life and guide us. My mom used to pray with me and tell me the exact same thing. I know she is watching from Heaven and would be happy that Dad is helping me to trust in God.

I traveled at an early age with my parents because my dad always wanted us with him whenever possible, even though we didn't see much of him on the trip. Dad encourages me by telling me that I will become more at ease with things that happen in life as I get older and develop my relationship with God. Dad explains, "The closer our relationship with

God, the more comfortable we will be in our everyday life." I understand what he is saying, but it is difficult sometimes to not be afraid. I am going to really try on this trip to be trusting and faithful that God will keep *Magic* and us safe.

My dad actually has the nerve to suggest that we not take *Magic.* When he suggests this, I feel really anxious. I depend on *Magic* to be with me most of the time, because I feel safer when we are together. I know that sounds weird, but something about her being with me is comforting. Maybe it is because she is a huge dog, and no stranger will come near me when she is with me. But it is more than that; I try to explain to my family. It's just that weird things happen sometimes when she is around…unexplained things, things that save my life. Everyone says it is my imagination.

One time, when we were on a camping trip with our church in San Diego, an incident happened that was really weird. Dad is really active at our church, when he is not on location filming a movie. We take advantage of all the trips our church plans, especially camping. We love to camp. Aunt Rue likes to come too, when she can get off duty.

The camping grounds had just been reopened after a few months of being closed on account of a vicious mountain lion attack in the area. This particular time, Aunt Rue came with us, and brought her rifle.

She said, "You can't be too careful when wild animals are involved." I think she only came along, because she knew my dad wouldn't bring a gun, and she was afraid for our safety. She would never admit it as she always tries to have a rough outer appearance, so no one will know she is an old softie.

The second day Dad, Aunt Rue, *Magic* and I went on a hike up Stone Wall Peak, a pretty easy trail. There were mountain lion warnings everywhere, but I wasn't worried because I had *Magic* with me, and Aunt Rue had a rifle. We left in the morning, while it was still somewhat cool and headed up to the peak. Aunt Rue went over the procedures. If we encountered a mountain lion, never run away from a wild animal, pick up rocks to throw, wave your arms and look as big as you can and make a lot of noise. *Yeah, Yeah, Yeah,* I thought.

"Switchback!" I yelled, as was the custom with my family when we were hiking. I was ahead of the rest of the family...just *Magic* and me. The trail was steep, rocky and slightly muddy. It must have sprinkled over night. Sometimes it does that in the mountains without warning. It was blue skies now though. I love hiking alone with *Magic*. It makes me feel like an explorer. God has really created a cool world for us to live in.

The air was moist with a musty smell, and the only sound was an occasional rustle in the bushes. The trail was long, narrow and winding. It felt like *Magic* and I were on a trail to heaven. Ahead were many, huge, pine trees and clear, blue skies. There were lots of large, granite boulders and feathery, emerald green ferns growing. It was creepy to think about what was lurking around in the ferns and thick trees beyond the trail. I felt like I was in the Garden of Eden, waiting for anything that may be lurking about. I couldn't hear my family behind me, but I knew that they had to be there. There was only one route on this trail.

Up ahead there was a giant, speckled boulder. There were lots of cool looking crevasses winding through it. I scrambled up the rock and plopped myself down facing the trail to wait for the rest of the slowpokes. *Magic* stood at the foot of it, with her head cocked to one side, looking at me like I was crazy.

"We'll just wait here for the rest of them." I said to *Magic* as I was investigating the crevasses in the rock with the smooth, thick walking stick I had picked up along the trail. She wagged her tail, like she always does when I talk to her.

I heard some rustling in the ferns off to the side of the boulder, and I figured it was either a lizard or a squirrel. I had seen a bunch of them since we had arrived at the campground. *Magic* stepped backwards. She stopped wagging her tail, and her ears perked up. She got rigid, which alarmed me as she was usually a very relaxed dog.

As I twisted to look back behind the boulder and into the ferns... I could instantly feel my heart engulf my whole body. My head started pounding furiously and I felt hot all over and froze... I found myself face to face with a vicious looking mountain lion that had emerged from the ferns. Its jagged teeth were barred and his pointy ears were flat against his head...the brown fur stood up on its neck. The lion crouched as if ready to pounce.

I slid down the jagged rock, fell on the ground on my knees, but immediately scrambled to get up. ***Magic*** was on alert, her ears back, and her tail up and stiff. Her eyes were glowing neon yellow and her fur was all-aglow too. I saw the enormous lion up on the rock and heard the low growling in its throat. It was balanced on the rock, crouched like it was ready to pounce.

I didn't know whether to run up the trail, or holler back to my family or pick up rocks to throw at the lion. Then... I remembered Aunt Rue's words. I held my walking stick high above my head in both my hands. Hiking up the trail...talking and laughing came Dad and Aunt Rue. I turned toward them and waved the stick side to side as a signal. My aunt saw me and stopped and grabbed my dad. We all stood, frozen, waiting for something to happen.

"Crackle, CRACK, CRACK," went the sound of thunder as a huge bolt of lightning struck the rock where the lion stood. The light was blinding and we all crouched on the ground...covering our heads. Silence fell, and we all slowly uncovered our heads, looking around cautiously as we stood up to see what had happened.

The lion was gone, and a fine mist became a pouring rain. I ran to ***Magic*** and she licked me and wagged her tail.

"What the heck was that all about?" Dad yelled as he and Aunt Rue raced toward ***Magic*** and me.

"Did you see the size of that cat?" I screamed.

"I wasn't aware that mountain lions were so huge!" yelled Aunt Rue.

When they got to me, we all hugged, while ***Magic*** jumped around.

"There was not a cloud in the sky!" exclaimed Aunt Rue.

"Did you see ***Magic***?" I yelled. "You must've seen her light up!"

Dad and Aunt Rue looked at each other with a curious expression on their face.

"What do you mean, 'light up'?" Aunt Rue asked.

"I can't believe you didn't see it" I responded. "She was all aglow, and her eyes were like neon yellow. It was amazing and bizarre. Could you believe the size of that cat? ***Magic*** was so brave. She stood right up to it. Did she scare the lion or did the lightening?"

My dad and Aunt Rue just looked at each other. Dad, who usually teased me about always claiming that ***Magic's*** eyes glow or that she has sparkly fur, didn't say a word. We all bent down and hugged and petted ***Magic.***

"Let's get outta here," pleaded Aunt Rue as she grabbed my dad and me by the arms. "Don't even think about going to look for that cat."

Dad and I went along quietly, lost in our own thoughts.

Maybe someday everyone will see ***Magic*** the way I do. I know that I am not imagining her special talents. Maybe it is because she is MY dog. Maybe she only shines for me. She always saves the day.

Aunt Rue gets vacation days and Grandma is in a whirlwind the whole week making arrangements for her upcoming party she has been asked to cater. Her two girlfriends, Phoebe and Mary, are going to cover for her, but she is still in a frenzy. She's really funny when she gets nervous. She tends to run around in circles, and my dad and Aunt Rue have to calm her down, before she develops an anxiety attack.

Anxiety attacks run in my family. I never could figure out how anyone could let anxiety or stress run his or her life. I worry when I travel, but not enough to let anxiety spoil my fun. The worst part about international travel is the long hours on the airplane. If the layover isn't long enough between connector flights, we have to run through the airport to catch the next plane, because international customs take so long. It is kinda fun running through the airport though, but not if it means ***Magic*** won't make the flight. The animals and baggage sometimes don't get on the same connector flight, if there is not enough time between the two flights. Strangely enough, ***Magic*** always makes the flight, even when our luggage doesn't.

Aunt Rue packs her detective stuff, like handcuffs, walkie-talkies, and her contact list. "You never know when you are going to be involved in a situation," she always says. I always hope for a situation because that is when ***Magic*** and I have the most fun. For some reason, we always manage to find ourselves in mysterious situations when we travel. Aunt Rue complains that she never gets to rest on vacation as something always pops up; but I know she is never truly happy unless she is tracking to solve some mystery, just like ***Magic*** and me.

My dad hauls out ***Magic's*** special cage for traveling. It is huge because of the regulations of the airlines. She also has a microchip in her skin with all the information about her vaccinations. We always give her a motion sickness pill because it makes her sleepy, so she can sleep the whole way. I hate having her in the cargo area, but to take her on the plane, she has to be able to fit under the seat. No way could *Magic* fit under the seat. She is used to traveling though, so she always manages to come through just fine.

"The flight is at 8:30 am, so we all need to be ready to go at 5:30 am. I know it's early, but with all our baggage and *Magic*, it will take a while to get checked in." Dad informs us at dinner.

We are all so excited; we know we will not sleep very well tonight anyway.

"I want to run through our plans, just to make sure everyone is clear on our flights, stops and procedures," Dad lectures. He always has to go over every detail, so no one messes up.

Magic sits on her haunches next to dad like she is listening to every word. Sometimes I think she knows exactly what were saying. We all have our questions, mostly about carry-on bags. We clean up and bring our entire luggage collection out to the garage to be loaded in the van.

It is hard to sleep when I am so excited. I lay in bed looking out the window of my room, which is lit up with the glow of the full moon. *Magic* lies next to the bed...head between her giant paws looking at me...the moonbeams streaming through the wind shine on *Magic*. She is vaguely sparkling. I say my prayers, without Dad tonight. I think he forgot.

I wonder how no one else sees how she sparkles. I wonder if my mom's dog had sparkled?

I fall right to sleep.

◆ ◆ ◆ ◆ ◆ ◆

Chapter Six
THE FLIGHT PLAN

"Bang, bang, bang, bang." Someone knocks on my door. It is still dark outside. *Magic* growls and then yelps as Aunt Rue opens my bedroom door and says, "Hey sleepyheads. Up and at 'em. It's show time."

Magic jumps on my bed and starts licking my face. I giggle trying to push her away. "Get off the bed, you big oaf," Aunt Rue says to *Magic* as she gently shoves her down. She grabs *Magic's* front paws, pulling them up to her waist and dances around with her singing, "We're off to Scotland to see the monster." *Magic* dances slightly sparkling, while my Aunt Rue laughs and hugs her. We all love *Magic*. I am so glad she gets to come too. Dad is really cool about letting us take *Magic* with us everywhere.

I am especially excited about going to Scotland as Aunt Rue and I have a fascination with the Loch Ness Monster. I know we are both hoping we will catch a glimpse of it. We are going to be staying next to Loch Ness in a town called Inverness. This town is in the highlands of Scotland. My Aunt and I had studied the monster for years. My mom was the one who got us started on it. She had a book on the sightings of the monster that she used to read with me and tell Aunt Rue about. My mom would be so excited to go. I pack the book to read again on the plane. I bet Aunt Rue misses my mom too.

My mom loved Aunt Rue. She is fun and has always had interesting stories, like the time she had to track down a man who was pretending to be someone else. It was really weird. He killed his family by cutting them up, and then he ran away. They never found him, but then his picture was on that T.V. show, *America's Most Wanted*, as a suspect in the murder of his family, which had happened years previous. Someone actually knew him living under some other name. Aunt Rue got to apprehend him and haul him back to justice.

I knew that Aunt Rue and I were going to have an adventure. We always do when we travel somewhere. That's why we have to take *Magic*. She always saves the day. We actually depend upon her.

"What is going on?" Dad asks as he walks into the room breaking into a smile from ear to ear when he sees the two dancing. "This will be a great trip. I am glad we are all going…but lets get cracking. We have to leave in 40 minutes."

I jump out of bed and hug *Magic* around her back and snuggle my face in her furry neck. "I love you, *Magic*." I whisper. Aunt Rue releases her paws and I tumble to the floor. *Magic* immediately starts licking my face, her favorite pastime.

"Oh you and that dog, "Aunt Rue warns. "I swear you two are like twins joined at the hip. See ya in the kitchen for breakfast. Hurry up. You know how your dad is about getting to the airport on time."

"Yeah, yeah, I'll beat you." I retort as I scramble up from the floor. *Magic* starts to jump around, as now she is in a very playful mood. She grabs my jammie bottoms and starts to tug. Now we are in a tug a war for my leg…

I always win, even if my jammies get ripped.

♦ ♦ ♦ ♦ ♦ ♦

Chapter Seven
HEAVEN BOUND

Since mom died, I always like flying in a plane, because I feel closer to her. I never tell anyone that because they would think I am weird. People don't know how it feels to lose your best friend and mom. Moms are irreplaceable. I don't fear death or worry about it either. I know death will take me to heaven to be with my mom. That is a weird way to feel too, but that is the way I feel. I still want to make her proud of me while I am here. That's why I think I love mysterious adventures so much.

She was a fiend for mysteries. She always watched detective shows on T.V. and read fantasy and mystery books. I must have inherited that from her. Of course, my dad is always on a quest for an adventure, which is why he is a filmmaker. That's why we have such a great time together. He is starting to include me more on his work trips, and that is really cool. He goes to some pretty neat places. Scotland is by far the best one he has come up with yet. Only 24 more hours until we reach Scotland. That is a long time, but I will sleep most of the way. The real adventure starts when we get there..

We finally arrive at the airport, and believe it or not, at 5:00 am it is already packed. What a crazy time to have to get to the airport. International travel always takes a long time, and you lose a day because of the time change. My dad always makes us stay awake when we finally get to wherever we are going, even though we lose a night's sleep. If you go to sleep when you arrive in the new country, you get all screwed up with the time. It makes you have really bad jet lag.

Thankfully, our flight has only one connection in New York and on to Edinburgh, Scotland. I really don't like it when we have to get off the plane somewhere on the East coast and catch another flight to our destination, usually in Europe. The airlines have a tendency to loose luggage, and changing flights makes loosing luggage easy. I would hate for them to loose *Magic*. I wish I could buy a seat for her next to me, but she is too big. She'll sleep the entire way. I don't think dogs get jet lag. My Aunt Rue and I will play cards, watch movies, and eat junk and sleep. Grandma will sleep. It won't be so bad.

Aunt Rue is shaking me, "Paul, Paul. We're here! Wake up!

My eyes, heavy and blurry from lack of sleep, focus on the seat in front of me and I remember where I am. We've arrived, I thought. I've got to get *Magic*. The panic sets in. I always get panicky when we arrive at our destination. I am anxious to get *Magic* out of her cage. It always takes so long after the plane lands to get to the luggage.

There she is. Her nose is sticking through the cage, tongue hanging out and panting. *"Magic"* I shout, as I dash over to her, weaving in and out of the half awake people wandering around the baggage claim area like zombies. Her eyes are sparkly. I know that she is okay. I turn to see if Aunt Rue is with me. She is next to me but just laughs when I mention *Magic's* eyes. She always thinks I imagine *Magic's* eyes sparkling.

"Hey there, you big mutt." Aunt Rue calls to *Magic*.

I'm already unlocking the cage to get her out. After greeting *Magic* and receiving her ritual bath, we are ready to go. Grandma also gets a tongue lashing from *Magic*. We wait and get the rest of the baggage, while my dad arranges for our car and driver. He always gets a company limo and driver, which is really cool. When we travel, we don't have to worry about much of anything, except that *Magic* is treated well. Everyone loves her, so we don't usually have trouble with anyone. She **is** special, and I guess people can sense that.

The usual briefing takes place between Dad and all of us, after we get in the limo, before we get on the road. He always gets nervous when we travel abroad. I always reassure him that all will be safe as long as *Magic* is with us, at which time he rolls his eyes and comments, "You and that dog."

Dad distributes walkie-talkie telephones to us. They are really cool. They are like telephones and walkie-talkies. The phones are tiny too. "Only use the phones when necessary. Do not take it out of your pocket unless you are going to use it. They are very expensive, so don't lose it or break it. Never turn it off."

Dad goes through his long list of rules. "Do not go anywhere by yourself. That means you too Ruthie. You may be tough, but you are small and in a foreign country where things are very different. Do not trust anyone with anything that you value. We will be meeting a lot of different types of people that will be hanging with us as filming a movie encompasses many different jobs. Some of the people I know well. Some I have had dealings with before, and some I have never met. These people are from different countries as well as we are. There will be a few that are from Scotland, but I don't know them. I will let you know whom I know and what I know of the people we meet. Do you guys understand?"

"Oh for the love of Pete!" Aunt Rue exclaims. (She always uses that expression when she is irritated). "I may be younger than you, but I am not stupid! Did you suddenly develop amnesia? Have you forgotten that I search out criminals and weirdoes for a living? Good grief, Noah, you are going to have to trust me a bit, because I will be hangin with Paul. I want to know that you are confident in me."

Grandma just sits there with a smirk on her face, watching the fight escalate. You know what they say about red heads? They are supposed to have quick and hot tempers. Well, when my dad and Aunt Rue disagree, the sparks fly.

"I'm sorry. I didn't mean to sound like a tyrant. You guys are the only family I have. I was thinking about that on the flight over, while I was praying for a safe flight and reflecting on what we are all embarking on. I started to think that maybe I was nuts to bring all of the people I care about on an adventure so far away, where anything could happen." Dad explains.

"We understand honey," Grandma responds to Dad, while Aunt Rue sits there with a disgruntled look on her face. "But you must remember," she says with a mischievous grin on her face, "We have *Magic* with us." *Magic* sits upright on her tail and back legs like she is begging, when she hears her name. Her tongue's panting so she looks like she's smiling. We all relax, and the tension is gone. Grandma always tries to lighten things up, and she usually succeeds. ***Magic*** just looks back and forth at us. Dad tells the driver to head on out.

We are finally on our adventure.

♦ ♦ ♦ ♦ ♦ ♦

Chapter Eight
MIDIEVAL TIMES

Everything looks like a castle in the city of Edinburgh, Scotland, even the new apartment buildings. The architects design and build everything to look medieval with gray stones and tower like structures on houses. I knew it would be cool, but this is awesome. We all 'ooh and ahh' as we check out the new surroundings. We make a lot of stops, as my dad has to check out different places he will be filming, and we grab something to eat at this really cool baked potato place. They serve gigantic potatoes with about twenty different toppings from which to pick.

The company my dad works for always rents an apartment for the film crew. I guess it is cheaper than a hotel. We are all expecting something small, since that is what everyone complains about when traveling abroad, and we are often confronted with small accommodations. America is one of the few countries with large hotel rooms. Grandma already reminded us about the accommodations and what to expect.

There are two parts in Edinburgh. There is the new part and the old part. The new part keeps evolving into a bigger medieval looking city, and the old part is a medieval city that has buildings from the 1300's. There is a huge castle in the middle of Edinburgh, where the queen and king used to go when there was an invasion. It is supposed to be the coolest place ever. The castle has been a royal residence, a prison and an army garrison. It is the most important castle in Scotland and has been at the center of a ton of wars. Now it is a national monument, museum and tourist attraction, which is why my dad is filming it.

Our apartment, for the first few days, is in the old part of Edinburgh, on a street called 'The Royal Mile'. This means we are going to be staying in a building that was built in the 1600's, a block from the Edinburgh castle. When we arrive, we discover that we have to climb up three flights of stairs with our entire collection of luggage to get to our apartment. Unfortunately, there are not many elevators in Scotland. The stairs are built in a spiral, and the whole enclosure and stairs is made of tan stone. At the top of the stairs, we drop our luggage in exhaustion. Dad opens the door.

"Check it out." Dad says. "This is like staying in a castle. It's huge. How many bedrooms are there? Look, there is a full kitchen," Dad exclaims as he walks around taking inventory of the accommodations. "Look at this bedroom. It has a stone tower in it."

Grandma, Dad and I check out the room with the tower, or curved wall in the one bedroom. It has a really low ceiling and no windows. There is a queen size bed and a dresser. There is a bathroom on the other side of the bed. The bathroom is fairly large and modern, compared to the room. Everything is super clean. We have noticed how clean everything is here in Scotland. We find another bedroom, which is a little more conventional. It is long and skinny with a window on the street. There are two twin beds in here placed end to end. There is another bathroom right across from the door we came through to enter the apartment.

"We are on the main street that leads down from the castle!" Aunt Rue exclaims as she looks out the window in the front room. "Check out all the action!"

I run to the window to see the street scene. The best part is that there is the annual August festival happening in Edinburgh called 'The Fringe Festival', which dad told us about when we were planning the trip. The whole town fills up with musicians, actors, comedians, marching bands, and artists who parade their wares and perform operas, plays and sword swallowing. I see why Aunt Rue is so excited while looking out onto the road. There are tons of people milling around on the street. Then we hear a bunch of booms, like fireworks going off. Soon after, an enormous crowd starts to roam down the street away from the castle.

My dad says, as he's checking out the stone walls in the front room, "The tattoo performance must have just ended.

The finale is probably fireworks. I hear it is fantastic. We will be attending it at some point on this trip. I will be filming, and you guys will be watching. Look at these walls. They are half stone and half wood. They must've tried to preserve as much of the stone as they could and repaired the rest with wood."

"Wow, you ain't kidding; there is a lot of action!" I yell. "Dad, Grandma, come see the people! What is a tattoo performance?"

Meanwhile, *Magic* is running around checking out all the rooms, sniffing in every corner. She must smell lots of unusual scents, since the building is so old.

Grandma shouts to my dad, "Noah, come look. We can watch all the festival activities from our window."

My dad answers me, "A tattoo performance refers to military bands performing their best songs and formations. I am sure that there will be a lot of bagpipes and kilts. It is supposed to be something to see."

We all stand and marvel out the window onto the street below. The windows reach across the entire front of the apartment, so there is plenty of room to stand and check it out. The windows crank open and have no screens, so we can hang out and look down the street to the big castle.

"What an amazing place!" I exclaim. "I don't ever remember any place having so much bizarre stuff to see. It really is like going back in time and being medieval. I've never seen anything so cool as Scotland!" I remark.

"I'm with you," says Aunt Rue.

Everyone is talking and pointing at all the sights. *Magic* finally joins us. She puts her front paws on the windowsill and looks out the window. She always wants in on the action. She is just like a person. I give her a big hug and pat her.

"You are the best." I whisper in her fur.

◆ ◆ ◆ ◆ ◆ ◆

◆ ◆ ◆ ◆ ◆ ◆

◆ ◆ ◆ ◆ ◆ ◆

Chapter Nine
THE 'MEET AND GREET' DISASTER

The first assignment my dad has, whenever we arrive on location for the film, is to meet with all the people involved. I look forward to this. There are usually other kids to play with. Sometimes they even bring their pets, like us. Everyone always loves *Magic*. There are so many people involved with filming a movie that it makes it hard to remember names. The director of the movie calls everyone together for an awesome meal so we can all meet. It is called a 'Meet and Greet.' The director always rents an amazing house wherever we go. I guess the director needs to have a lot of space to get everyone together.

Grandma wants to shop instead of attending the 'Meet and Greet', so she is staying at our apartment. She is a big shopper. She always finds cool stuff. Everything looks medieval in this city, so I am excited to see what she finds today. Aunt Rue and I are anxious to see if this weird kid and his dad are going to be at the 'Meet and Greet'. This scary kid's dad is a special effects guy, who lives in Australia and mostly films horror films. He is hired to participate in this film. Sometimes he brings his son, Judas. I try and stay away from him. I convince Dad that he has to let me bring *Magic* tonight for protection; Besides Grandma is going shopping, and *Magic* can't stay by herself in a foreign country. That would be rude.

Aunt Rue, dad and I eagerly arrive at this huge, gray stone castle taking a cobblestone road over an ancient stone bridge. It is a moat type effect. The castle is surrounded by enormous trees and gardens loaded with colorful flowers and paths leading everywhere through the grounds. It almost looks like a maze. Aunt Rue and I are excited to explore the castle and grounds as quickly as we can because it is going to be dark soon.

We proceed up a stone walkway to find ourselves in a foreboding, stone tunnel, which leads us to a massive stone courtyard with plants climbing up all sides of the castle. Aunt Rue and I look at each other.

Aunt Rue comments, "This is right out of *Frankenstein.*"

My dad is amused. "This is going to be some experience with you two melodramatic fiends." He replies.

Magic starts barking. We all turn to observe what she sees and there she is crouched and growling, edging forward towards a dark, dreary archway leading off the courtyard.

"Oh no…now you have to get in on the act!" My dad exclaims to **Magic**.

In front of us stand two amazing stone doors with stained glass and gold trim in the middle. The etching looks like some kind of family crest with green and red and gold in the emblem. Many families in Scotland once belonged to groups called 'clans'. The clans were mostly members of a family or people who hung together and had been friends for generations. Each clan lived in different areas of the highlands or mountain area and was always fighting with one another. They developed their own family crest or coat of arms, along with their own tartan patterns.

Tartan is a plaid material used to make kilts. Scottish men used to wear kilts and often still do for special events. They are like plaid vests and skirts and are worn with knee socks. They are really funky looking, Each clan had their own particular tartan plaid, which would help members identify each other, so they wouldn't kill the wrong person. They were always fighting in medieval times. I am sure glad I don't have to wear a kilt.

Aunt Rue exclaims, "Wow, is this guy married?"

Dad and I laugh. Aunt Rue is not too interested in getting married because of her work, so it is funny to hear her say that.

Dad informs her, "Yeah, **SHE'S** married," as he rings the chimes.

"She has twin girls, who I think are going to be here. They are thirteen years old, I believe. Just right for you." Dad teases me.

"Oh yeah…girls. Just what I need to get in my way," I reply.

"I think she has a boy about your age too, and she told us she was bringing them this trip and encouraged us to bring our kids to keep hers occupied," adds Dad.

"Yeah, you just wait. The girls will be chasing after you before you know it, and you will be liking it," teases Aunt Rue.

"Let's change the subject." I reply.

"This is way cool," says Aunt Rue. "A little creepy, but cool."

Dad comments, "Boy, these producers know how to live."

An extremely tall, buffed out, bald man in a black tuxedo answers the door and very stiffly invites us in. He looks questioningly at *Magic.*

"Oh, she's a good and quiet dog. She won't bother anyone. After I meet everyone, I'll take her outside to play." I say pleadingly. The butler just raises his eyebrows, stands aside and motions for us to enter. Aunt Rue and I look at each other and try to stifle our laughter.

Straight ahead is a colossal room with an amazingly high ceiling. Dark, carved wood at the edges of the ceiling borders pastel paintings of angelic looking figures floating in a blue sky with white clouds. Huge, old styled paintings of horses and people hunting and a couple of portraits decorate the walls. There are long, carved, dark wood tables along the sides of the room with gold lamps and white and black marble statues of animals and people placed on them. In the middle of the huge room are several sitting areas with red and gold velvet sofas. They are real fancy with carved, dark wooden legs and trim. Nearby are gold, iron, and glass top tables where people are setting their drinks and snacks. Waiters in black tuxedos wander around with silver trays carrying colorful drinks and appetizers. Everyone seems to be having a good time.

Suddenly, *Magic* starts to growl softly. I spot a gigantic, furry, black dog across the room. I pet *Magic's* head to calm her down.

Aunt Rue is enthralled with this magical room, looking around, her mouth slightly agape, and admiring the general awesomeness. I grab her arm. She looks at me startled, with a questioning look.

"What?" She says in an irritated tone.

"Look, over there," I motion with my head. "See the enormous black dog,? I think, that is Judas next to him," I whisper.

"Well, well. I sure wouldn't want to mess with either of them. You say the boy's name is Judas? That's weird," Aunt Rue says quietly. "He looks like the grim reaper with his black ensemble, skinny body, white face and black greasy hair. I wonder where he's hiding his scythe."

"I think his weapon would be that nasty looking dog," I whisper back.

"*Magic* started growling, when she saw the black dog," I whisper quietly.

"I don't blame her," whispers Aunt Rue. "It looks like the devil in wolves' clothing."

"Don't you mean sheep's clothing?" I question.

"Are you kidding? There is nothing soft and furry about those two," she chuckles.

I start looking around for other kids my age, while Aunt Rue checks out the room. I spy a couple of boys about my age hanging with the adults. Oh, and I spot two girls. They don't look like twins. I hope those aren't two more girls other than the twins.

A few minutes later, the massive, bald butler walks up to me and says, "The doors to the patio and gardens are this way." He motions for me to follow him. I guess that's his way of telling me to get the dog out. Aunt Rue quickly joins me. As we pass by Judas and his dog, the butler motions for them to follow as well. Luckily, there are many people between us, so the dogs don't get close. I am worrying about a dogfight. I could only imagine the havoc that would cause with all this fancy furniture and drinks everywhere. That could be a scene I prefer to avoid.

Aunt Rue follows me out. "I want to check out the gardens anyway," She comments. "I don't see anyone too interesting in there."

The butler leads us out onto a massive covered patio with a stone floor and hedge walls. It is cool how the hedge grew thick and tall to create walls. There are lots of sitting areas with stone benches and small round tables made of iron with glass tops and iron chairs. No one is out here. It is cool outside, as is the norm from what we have observed so far in Scotland. *Magic* is pulling on the leash and snarling at the ominous, black dog, which Judas is struggling to contain.

The butler exclaims in his Scottish accent, "Well, I would hope you would take those dogs in opposite directions. They do not look to be too fond of one another."

I stare down at *Magic* and her eyes are sparkling with a neon glow. Glancing at the black dog, I note his eyes are blazing red. I glare at Judas and quickly call *Magic* away, tugging at her leash, and we go off through one of the garden entrances. Aunt Rue follows me quickly. We just want to get away from that menacing dog.

"Wow, that could've been disastrous. What a mean looking dog 'gothic boy' has!" Aunt Rue exclaims. "You say his name is Judas? So weird."

"Did you see *Magic*'s and the other dog's eyes?" I ask frantically.

"I was too busy looking at his teeth!" Aunt Rue whispers. "I am positive that we will have to stay away from those two."

Aunt Rue and I explore the gardens, which are like a perfectly groomed maze with statues of naked cherub type looking creatures, three-tiered fountains and large, colorful flowers everywhere. The flowers are huge, and there are so many. The path is cobblestone. The hedges are about six feet tall, with the intermittent statues. I have never seen so many huge flowers. They are everywhere in lots of different colors.

"We better leave breadcrumbs so we can find out way back," jokes Aunt Rue.

I laugh but realize that she might be right. "Let's turn back. It's getting a little dark. The other dog will be gone, and we can hang out on the patio," I plead.

"Sounds good to me," agrees Aunt Rue.

Around the next corner, we come face to face with Judas and his massive, midnight-black, furry dog. We stop abruptly, frozen. We stare at each other, while the dogs crouch low and start to growl.

"You must be Paul. I remember you and your pansy dog too." Smirks Judas. "You just keep that mutt away from my 'Goliath'. You will come to see that he is named appropriately. What was your dog's name again? Margie or some stupid girly name, wasn't it?"

At that, *Magic* stands tall and lunges forward snarling at Goliath whose eyes are radiating red, while snarling with big globs of slobber dripping off his mouth. He is much bigger than *Magic*, but I can tell that he is threatened.

Magic keeps pulling and wanting to lunge at Goliath. Judas finally steps forward, pulling the giant Goliath back while trying to position himself in between the dogs.

"Call off your pitiful mutt before I let Goliath tear her apart." Judas yells, fear in his face and eyes.

Magic backs off when Judas steps towards her. It was like she didn't want to hurt him. Aunt Rue threatens, "You better mind yourself as well as your dog. You have no idea who you are dealing with."

"What a wimp. Your mom has to stick up for you. Waa, Waa, Waa." Judas retorts angrily.

"You just wait! We'll show you!" I exclaim.

Magic suddenly turns and leads us away down one of the paths. After we are clear of Judas and his dog, *Magic* stops, turns and sits down and looks at us. Aunt Rue and I look at each other, laugh and embrace our brave *Magic.*

"Did you see Goliath's eyes?" I exclaim to Aunt Rue as we stand there recovering.

"The eyes again?" She questions. "What is with you and these dogs' eyes? I never see what you describe. Maybe it is the way the light hits them. Besides…like I said before, I was too occupied looking at his teeth. Both of them were very scary. I didn't know *Magic* had it in her!"

"That was really scary. Did you pray? I didn't know what was going to happen." I confide in Aunt Rue.

"You better believe I prayed. God was watching over us, as usual. I just wish he would prevent more harrowing things from happening rather than save us after we're scared to death. But I guess life would be pretty boring, if that was how it went," Aunt Rue confesses.

I know that if she did not see the eyes, she definitely did not notice the way the head of Goliath started to puff up, with bumps forming over his ears. That is when *Magic* started to glow and come unglued and when Judas stepped between the dogs with a pretty terrified expression on his face. I was mortified and could not move or react, so I just prayed to God to help us instead. I don't think that I have ever been so scared.

We return to the patio, experiencing many weird sounds along the way. I am still a little nervous. I sure am glad that *Magic* and Aunt Rue are here. Aunt Rue is always brave and courageous. *Magic* is the bravest dog I have ever seen. She can also be the scariest.

We settle in on the patio observing the activities going on inside. Everyone is talking and laughing, shaking hands, eating, drinking and mingling. It sure is a different environment inside the castle than it is out here, I thought.

"We should take turns going in and meeting some of these people," Aunt Rue offers.

"Yeah, I guess you're right. Or we can wait 'til Dad comes out and gets us, or brings those he wants us to meet." I say hopefully.

"Any other dreams you wanna share?" Teases Aunt Rue.

"You go first." I reply.

"OK, but stay put. If you feel anxious or concerned, just come in. The butler will have to get over it," responds Aunt Rue.

"OK," I agree.

Aunt Rue pats *Magic* on the head, "You watch out over our Paul now." She coos to *Magic*. *Magic* turns and looks at me and wags her tail, dusting the ground with its massive broom like quality. Aunt Rue and I exchange glances and smiles.

"I'll be fine." I lie to her, still apprehensive about future encounters.

◆ ◆ ◆ ◆ ◆ ◆

◆ ◆ ◆ ◆ ◆ ◆

◆ ◆ ◆ ◆ ◆ ◆

CHAPTER TEN
IMAGINATION?

"You should've seen *Magic,* Dad. She was awesome!" I exclaim as we leave the party and are heading out to our limo. "I thought she was going to tear that huge, black monster apart."

"Whoaaa there Paul. I leave you three alone for 30 minutes and you manage to come close to getting killed?" Dad questions.

"Well, first of all, it was more than an hour that we had to get into that much trouble. Secondly, that boy Judas' dog is a killer!" I yell.

"Settle down. What boy and dog?" asks Dad.

"Didn't you see him? The tall skinny boy dressed all in black with creepy white skin and his massive, black, evil looking dog? He was in the first room that the butler led us into." I respond.

"I was busy trying to meet and greet people that I will be working with. I think I remember seeing a young boy in all black, but mostly, I noticed the monster dog. So that dog was the 'Goth boy's'? Now that I think of it, I noticed you all walking out with the butler," replies dad.

"That was Judas and Goliath." I reply excitedly.

"Are you kidding me?" Dad asks chuckling. "How original is that?"

"If you met them face to face, you wouldn't think it was a laughing matter," chides Aunt Rue.

Dad turns and looks at Rue laughing, "You too?"

"This is no laughing matter. You should've seen that dog in action. He wanted to rip *Magic* apart!" Aunt Rue exclaims. "He probably wanted to rip Paul and me apart as well."

"*Magic* stood right up to those two evil souls and they were scared. Weren't they Aunt Rue?" I say to dad and Aunt Rue.

"That evil looking boy put a stop to the fight for some reason. I would venture to guess that he was afraid that *Magic* might do some damage," replies Aunt Rue.

"You should've seen Goliath's eyes dad. The were blazing red, like lava." I exclaim.

"The eyes again, huh? Hey Ruthie, did you get a load of these lava eyes?" Dad teases.

"Oh, the eyes... Well, Paul did mention them, but like I told him, I was too busy looking at the huge, sharp teeth." Exclaims Aunt Rue. "They were something...almost razor looking."

"Here we are. Hello James. We are ready to go back to the hotel. That is if we don't get attacked by some vicious boy and dog," Dad teases.

Aunt Rue and I look at each other and shake our heads as we get in the limo. I let *Magic* jump in first. She knows to go to the back.

"You are so annoying, Noah. You just wait. We'll see who will be running scared before this trip is up," warns Aunt Rue.

"Oh, come on you two. I am sure it probably was a close call, but the castle and the creepy surroundings most likely had something to do with supplying the terror factor to the whole incident. Particular surroundings can stimulate our imaginations," reassures dad. "I know there are more teenagers that are supposed to be on this trip. That is why I thought it would be kinda nice for you to come this time. You probably won't see this 'vicious boy and his colossal dog' much. From the way you describe him, he seems like the kind of guy who does not have a lot of friends. Besides, maybe you can influence him and his dog. You know... be kind, friendly...try to show him positive behavior. He and his dog might realize the errors of their ways."

"Oh yeah, I am sure that will happen. I can't even get within 10 feet of him and his dog without threats of ripping us apart. I think I will pass on trying to be kind and friendly." I respond indignantly.

Just as we are about to pull away, I spy Judas and Goliath lurking around next to some tall, dense, dark hedges. They are hiding in the shadows watching us.

"Look, Dad, over there…to the right…by those hedges. Judas and his dog are spying on us." I exclaim.

"You probably scared him. Can't a guy hang around without looking suspicious?" Dad replies. "I have to say, though…his dog is definitely massive. I think I would be hesitant to even pet him, even when he's in a good mood."

"Why are you sticking up for him? I am your son." I say angrily.

"I am not sticking up for him. I just want us all to have a good time and not go looking for trouble or ridiculous adventures. Maybe you just started off on the wrong foot. Let's give it a chance before we jump to conclusions. OK? Let's try and keep our imaginations at bay," Dad pleads.

Aunt Rue, *Magic* and I sit quietly in the back seat. I can't wait to see Grandma and tell her about the incident. I know she will be interested in the unfolding adventure. While we are all silently lost in our own thoughts, *Magic*…looking out the back window…suddenly barks. We all jump.

"OK then," Dad teases. "We are all in agreement."

◆ ◆ ◆ ◆ ◆ ◆

CHAPTER ELEVEN
GRANDMA'S PREDICTION

"So, how was the first meeting? Did everyone seem to be congenial?" Grandma asks back in our apartment.

"It is hard to make that judgment on a 'Meet and Greet' cocktail hour," replies dad. "The castle where the event was held was amazing."

"Oh, really. A castle? Did you see any interesting men, Ruthy?" questions Grandma. Grandma is always trying to play matchmaker with Aunt Rue. For some reason, Grandma wants her to get married and settle down. She thinks Aunt Rue's life is too adventurous and dangerous for a young woman.

"Don't start playing matchmaker, mom. Paul and I were too busy trying to avoid this vicious boy and his monster dog."

"Please, (dad chuckles) are we going to start that again?" Dad responds.

"What's this all about? Was there another boy with his dog?" Grandma questions.

"You should have seen what happened, Grandma! We could've been torn apart…but the boy and his massive dog backed down…after *Magic* started her sparkling and glowing." I exclaim.

"Honestly, Paul. You and *Magic* must have some weird connection, because I never see this glowing stuff," responds Aunt Rue. "But I did think we were going to get torn apart. I am not going to lie. It was pretty scary. As usual, we had an angel protecting us."

"You said you didn't see Goliath's red eyes either. I swear I saw his head swell up too…like he was growing horns." I shout. "You really have to pay more attention, so you will see these changes take place. I couldn't be imagining it."

"Whoa Paul…you are taking this into a whole other dimension. Now you saw horns?" Well, I don't know about all that. It all sounds too creepy for me. I hope we don't' run into them again. I don't want to see red blazing eyes and horns on a vicious animal." Aunt Rue whines.

"Well, Noah, did you see any men that might be prospects for Ruthy?" Grandma brings it back around to this line of questioning.

Aunt Rue rolls her eyes and tries to change the subject. "Did you find any interesting souvenirs, mom?"

"Don't try to change the subject. This would be a perfect time to meet someone interesting. Besides, Noah said that there were going to be several teenagers…so Paul will have friends to play with, which will free you up to enjoy yourself and maybe make some new friends of your own," exclaims Grandma.

"Would you stop, mom. If God wants me to find someone, I will. When it is time, I am sure God will give me a sign. I appreciate that you want me to find someone, and it would be nice to meet someone really great…but it will happen in God's time," reasons Aunt Rue. "I gave up on that quest a couple of years ago, because I know that things happen at the right time."

"As a matter of fact," says Dad, "there are supposed to be several eligible bachelors here, which is partly why I invited you on this trip, Ruthy."

"What is this, a conspiracy?" Aunt Rue laughs.

"I don't know whether I would call it a conspiracy, but there is no reason to ignore the possibilities of bringing people together. It can't hurt to try." Dad responds calmly. "Actually, there are two single men, that I know of, who are involved with this production. One is named Adino…a film guy from Greece. You know the type…tall, dark and handsome with an exotic accent. The production design guy from England, Josiah, is also single. He is tall, blonde with an English accent. He has a girl, who is about Paul's age, so we might have romantic matches all around."

"Very funny. You are as bad as mom, although they don't sound like your typical boring detectives that I always have to hang around. Exotic is good," teases Aunt Rue.

"Well, you can count me out," replies Paul. "I did not come on this trip to hassle with girls. I want to have some adventures and excitement…especially in Scotland with castles and the Lock Ness monster." Everyone moans at the Loch Ness monster comment. They all know how obsessed I am with the claims of sightings of the creature.

"I have a funny feeling that this trip is going to be a whole lot more than just an excursion in Scotland. Between Paul and *Magic's* opposition to the other boy…his dog and all the eligible bachelors…not to mention the whole raft of teenagers…we are definitely in for some real adventure and mischief. God be with us." Grandma prays.

Grandma forgot to mention the Loch Ness monster.

◆ ◆ ◆ ◆ ◆ ◆

Chapter Twelve
DUNGEONS AND DEMONS
AT EDINBURGH

Finally, we get to go on a cool excursion and watch my dad film. I am not planning on watching him film the whole time, because I want to explore the castle. We are going to the Edinburgh Castle, which is in the center of Edinburgh, Scotland. My dad told me all about it on the plane over. He has this book with really cool pictures that we looked at and read. We always want to know about what we are going to visit before we go. It makes everything more interesting, and then you can visualize what was happening back in the old days better.

The Edinburgh castle is built on an extinct volcano called Castle Rock. The castle looms above the middle of the city with its huge, gray stone walls. It is visible from all parts of the city. People have lived in Edinburgh since the Bronze Age, which was around 850 BC. The royal castle has been here since the 12ᵗʰ century. It will be an awesome medieval experience. *Magic* gets to come, because we will all be in there before the crowds arrive. That is what is so cool about traveling with my dad. We get to explore all the really cool places before the public is allowed in.

I read that this castle is haunted. It doesn't surprise me, as it was originally built in 1018 AD. It is the most haunted place in Scotland. There are many dark dungeons where prisoners were locked up and forgotten. There are only a couple of dungeons that are opened to tourists. A few hundred years ago, secret tunnels were discovered deep underground running from the castle to other places in the city. A piper boy was sent down to investigate, instructed to constantly play his bagpipes, so those above could chart his progress through the tunnels. When the playing suddenly stopped, they went and searched for the piper boy, but he had vanished. His ghostly pipes can still be heard playing in the castle to this day, so they say. It is probably just a fabricated ghost story to make tourists want to visit the castle, but it is still creepy.

There are all kinds of jewels and crowns and ornate relics displayed here too in the throne room. The 'Stone of Destiny' is kept at the castle with the crown jewels of Scotland. The stone is the traditional coronation stone of all Scottish and English Kings and Queens and has been fought over by England and Scotland over the ages. Those areas will probably be off limits. I really want to take *Magic* and explore the depths of the castle. It will be scary. I don't care much about seeing the jewels, but I am sure Aunt Rue will want me to see them.

There is a palace down the road from the Edinburgh castle called Holyrood. The street between them is called "The Royal Mile," which is where our apartment is. The Holyrood palace was where the Royalty stayed most of the time. When there was a threat of war, all the royalty would move to the main Edinburgh castle in the middle of town, where we will be today.

The Edinburgh castle is a fortress that would protect the King, Queen and other royal attendants when they were threatened. All around the edges of the castle are huge canons facing out towards the city and water. Aunt Rue assures me that I can climb on the canons. It will be a good picture. The canons are called Mons Meg made about 1450. The cannon fired huge solid stone cannonballs…three times the size of your head. Each weighed 400 pounds and could be fired as far as 2 miles. The cannons are really cool. The castle is enormous…like a little city. The castle is not pretty and does not look like a regular castle. It looks more like a fortress, huge, gray and clunky. There is nothing elegant about it. Most castles have round, pointy structures that look gothic, but not this castle. It is very sprawling and rather ugly with square buildings. I like it. It is very daunting and spooky.

We split up, so *Magic* and I can go explore, while the others check out where dad is going to be filming. I wander into one of the dungeon areas where tourists can go. I have to squeeze through this huge rock door propped open with another huge stone. People must've been small back then. There are about 4 giant stairs going down steeply, and it is really dark and smells like wet stone. I carefully feel my way down the stairs, thinking it is pretty dangerous for tourists. As I am poking around, making my way to the other end of the dungeon waiting for my eyes to adjust, I look in disbelief at the accommodations. There are cots three high along each side, twelve in all. It is a very narrow space. The cots hang on cords from the ceiling, one on top of the other. It must've smelled bad, when it was filled to capacity. The cots are the only things in here. It feels eerily still.

Suddenly, I smell the scent of something strange and hideous. It is the scent of something dead or living with death. *Magic* starts to growl her unusual, low pitched, pensive growl, which indicates there is trouble. Uh oh… I think cautiously…this doesn't sound good… I swing around to see where she is…and standing in the shadows at the end of the dungeon area… I see two gigantic, fiery red eyes… I gasp.

I whisper, "*Magic*, let's go." The beast with fiery eyes makes this ear piercing sound…between a growl and a scream, and simultaneously its jagged jaw of razor sharp, red, glowing teeth appear… I jump back, stumbling. *Magic* puffs up to an enormous size and starts to glow brighter neon yellow then I have ever seen her glow before. The sound that escapes her is blood curdling, and she lunges forward in all her glory. She looks like a brilliant fireball in full armor… The noise is unbearable as the two collide.

"*Magic,* Let's get out of here!" I scream as I try and feel my way back…hearing the macabre screaming.

I turn and scramble out…stumbling up the stairs and turn to look for *Magic.* I pray that she is OK. I look around for my dad or someone to help me get *Magic.* She suddenly appears, after I emerge from the opening of the dungeon. She looks normal again. I hug her and look at her, searching for any injuries or changes. I am in shock at what just happened. That monstrous, grotesque creature or demon trying to murder *Magic,* while screaming the most frightful sound I have ever heard. I know now that *Magic* is not just some dog…she is a force to be reckoned with. I put her leash on and direct her away from that dungeon from Hell.

"We gotta find dad and Aunt Rue," I whisper out of breath. We turn the corner and there they are.

"You'll never believe what just happened." I whisper, trembling.

"Calm down, Paul," Dad, Aunt Rue and Grandma all chime in.

"You and that dog are gonna get us tossed out of here. Come along and we'll talk calmly while we go look at the throne rooms with all the jewels," soothes Dad.

"Wi...wi...will it be in a dark ca...ca...cave?" I stammer.

"Whatever has got into you?" Aunt Rue croons as she puts her arm around me and looks at **Magic** and me. "Come on you two. Tell me what happened. Let's go sit down on those benches by the canons,"

As we walk away in a worried huddle, the door to the dungeon slams shut with a creak and a boom. Dust puffs out from all around the ground. The rock holding it open was gone. Immediately...a couple of guys, who work at the castle, run over to the dungeon door, look at each other and stare at the door. One guy gets on the walkie-talkie...and they both back up from the door.

We all watch... I...knowing something fierce just happened. The rest of my family stops...stares back at the door with questioning faces.

"This place is starting to creep me out!" exclaims Aunt Rue.

♦ ♦ ♦ ♦ ♦ ♦

Chapter Thirteen
THE ROYAL MILE

"Well, all in all it was a successful filming session. That castle is amazing." Dad exclaims, as we are getting ready to go to dinner. "Well, it was successful except for the mishap with you, Paul."

"I am sorry dad. I shouldn't have gone exploring a haunted castle by myself. That was dumb. It is a lot less scary when something really horrifying and creepy happens, if you have someone with you. That way there are two who are deciding on what to do, and people are more apt to believe what happened," Paul explains.

"It is not that I don't believe you, Paul. I just think that you have an active imagination," replies Dad.

"Really, you guys. It was like the dungeon tasted like hate…and smelled like death…and then the sounds…and *Magic,*" I plead.

"Tomorrow we are going to that festival, right?" Aunt Rue questions trying to change the subject.

"Yup, and it should be cool. We already saw some of it from our apartment. The festival is on 'The Royal Mile' where we're staying. Up and down the street are the vendors, performers and artists, along with all the people we saw milling around. In the park down past the castle are more attractions. I can't wait to see the sword shallower. We will be meeting a bunch of the film crew tonight for dinner at this restaurant near the castle. Hopefully, the other kids will be there and Paul can meet them…and, you… Ruthie can meet the eligible bachelors." Dad responds excitedly.

"Oh, so you're gonna start that again," Aunt Rue whines.

"I saw Ruthie speaking with some tall, dark and handsome Greek guy after the episode with Paul at the castle," taunts Grandma.

"Really? I must've missed that," teases Dad.

"Well you didn't miss much. He said 'Hi', who are you with? My name is Adino, and are you going to be at the dinner tonight?" Aunt Rue drones.

"Never-the-less, he did approach you," retorts Dad, "and, if you are cordial and try to be interesting and not scare him off, he might accompany you to the Tattoo performance at the Edinburgh Castle."

"Oh, that's right. That is when the military bands have a performance, isn't it?" I inquire.

"Yeah. You remembered, even after all the drama today." Dad says with sarcasm.

"Actually, he wasn't bad looking. Not that I am in the market," adds Aunt Rue. "Wait a minute. Are you trying to pawn me off?

"Oh, you caught on, huh?" Dad laughs. "Of course not, sis. I just feel kinda guilty neglecting you, Paul and mom, since it has been awhile since we have been on vacation together. It is just that I have massive filming to do, and I want to make sure you guys are having fun."

"Noah, do I detect a tad of unselfishness shining through?" Aunt Rue teases as she knocks my dad's baseball cap off, which always irritates him. He has a thing about wearing his hat. He has a million of them. Everywhere he goes, he gets a baseball cap.

Grandma and I laugh, as we know that Aunt Rue will probably scare any eligible bachelors away with her hard-core detective personality. She can be deceiving, because she is petite and pretty, I guess, but really can size up people and situations.

"What will we do with **Magic** tonight?" I ask.

"Believe it or not, I have already thought about that. I spoke with Rachel, the director, and she informed me that it was fine to bring the dog. Evidently…we have a large room, so it won't be a problem," Dad replies.

"What about Goliath?" I exclaim.

"Oh, for Pete's sake!" warns dad. "I am sure that, if Goliath is hanging around, there won't be a problem. If there's a problem, we will just have to leave."

"Better he leave. Maybe he won't come." I reply hopefully. "Where is this restaurant?"

"It is conveniently on 'The Royal Mile' by the Edinburgh Castle. I thought it might be at the castle we went to for the first 'Meet and Greet'. You know…the one where Mr. Goth and Goliath almost ate you for dinner?" Dad teases.

Grandma reassures, "Paul, don't worry about that young man and his vicious dog. If he is the type you describe, he won't be caught dead at a social function that consists of sitting, eating and being polite with others. Above all…ignore your dad." Grandma gives Dad a disapproving look.

"You're probably right." I concede.

"Let's not let the thought of him and his evil side kick spoil our expectations and fun here in our medieval adventure," reassures Aunt Rue.

"The only thing I have been warned about is the food," comments dad.

"What do you mean?" Aunt Rue asks.

"Yeah." Grandma and I ask with concern.

"Well, some say that the food here in Scotland is a little sketchy." Dad warns.

"What do you mean 'sketchy'?" Aunt Rue asks cautiously.

"There is not a whole lot of a variety, and some of the choices are things that we're not used to. They serve things like haggis, a typical Scottish dish made with oatmeal and intestines; fish, which is supposed to be good; different cuts of meat from the cows, like tongue, oxtail soup and other delicacies, which we are not familiar with. I am told that the soup or stew is usually outstanding, along with the fish. You probably don't want to try a hamburger. The beef is different than ours in the U.S. But we are not here for the food, right? We are here for this amazing medieval adventure!" Dad explains.

"Just keep telling yourself that when it's time to eat, big brother," replies Aunt Rue as she pats him on the back.

The restaurant, like all the other buildings, is totally medieval looking. It is shaped like a castle with gray stones and winding stairs and a rounded window halfway up. Everything is gray stone. It is cool. We go up a flight of stone stairs into a restaurant that looks like someone's house or rather castle. In the back is a larger room where I recognize some of the people from the first party. There are a few of the film crew here, whom we saw earlier today at the castle.

"Thank the Lord, I do not see 'the devil and his spawn,'" Aunt Rue whispers to me.

"Me either… I hope they just aren't late," I respond.

"So where is Mr. Goth and his dog, 'Goliath'? Dad asks.

Aunt Rue and I shoot him a vicious look.

"Okay already, okay already," Dad surrenders, hands up like Aunt Rue and I are about to arrest him.

Aunt Rue warns in a whisper, "Everybody act natural…people are noticing we are here. We don't want to arouse any suspicions."

Dad responds, "Suspicions about what? You two nutcases?"

"You're asking for it now… Oh hi there… I guess we're not the first ones here," Aunt Rue covers up our argument as she greets the tall, dark and handsome Greek guy Grandma had been raving about.

Dad elbows me and smiles.

"Hey look, Paul. I see those twin girls across the room. Let's go sit at that table," Dad says as he puts his arm across my shoulders and propels me across the room towards the twins.

"Hey Dad," I say as I slow way down and turn out of his grip. "Will *Magic* be able to come with us to the Tattoo performance?"

"Sure. It takes place on the outside area of the castle. It is quite the show, evidently. They light up the castle as well. Hopefully, you will make friends tonight at dinner, and you all can go together to the performance tomorrow. Rachel…you know…the director…suggested that possibility. She said that the limo driver could take all you young people and drop you off there. If that comes about…just be sure and stay out of trouble. I don't want my boss to think I'm a flake," replies Dad.

"What if I don't like the kids?" I question.

"Since when do kids not like kids?" Dad asks. "Come on, let's go. We are making a spectacle of ourselves."

"Yeah, I have met a couple of them before. It will be fine." I answer, trying to be cooperative. I don't want dad to decide it is not a good idea to bring me on these trips. Next trip, though, I hope he lets me bring

Jacob and Micah. We will all be almost 15 next summer. They are my best friends, and we really know how to explore stuff together. They get *Magic* too.

They believe me when I tell them how *Magic* glows.

◆ ◆ ◆ ◆ ◆ ◆ ◆

Chapter Fourteen
MAGICAL INTRODUCTIONS

Introductions at the restaurant are easy enough. Of course, everyone wants to meet *Magic* first. They all love her and want her to sit next to them. She is always a big hit. This trip will be more interesting with all these kids my age here. As it turns out, there are several eligible bachelors for Aunt Rue to meet. I learn all about the eligible men while we eat. I am glad the parents let us sit by ourselves. Maybe hanging with these kids will be more exciting and fun than I had thought.

I met Jeremiah a long time ago, when mom and I went with dad on a film trip He is here with his father, Barnabas…single…who is the special effects guy. Jeremiah is 13. He's tall, has spiky brown hair and is really funny. They are from Los Angeles like us.

Jesse is really cool. He was born in Madagascar and lives in England and is 16 years old. He's really tall, stocky, and dark skinned with tons of curly black hair. He has traveled everywhere with his dad, so has lots of cool stories. The twin girls, Anastasia and Delilah, the director's daughters, seem to be interested in him, thankfully. Jesse doesn't seem to mind being the oldest. His dad, Peter is the makeup artist. He too is single.

Then there is Adam, the director's son, who is 13. He is tall, skinny and awkward. He has brown hair and does not look like his twin sisters. Come to think of it, his twin sisters do not look anything alike either. I guess they must be fraternal twins, or non-identical. That means that they were born about the same time but did not share the same sack in their mom's belly. It is all weird to me. My grandma always tells me weird facts like that. They are 15 years old. One of the twins, Anastasia is tall, has long, dark brown hair, is thin and looks athletic. She is really chatty and funny. The other twin is Delilah. She is short, has short blondish hair and is a little chubby. She is funny too. They tease each other a lot. They barely look like sisters, let alone twins. They live in Los Angeles too.

There is another teenage girl, Sarah, and she is English and lives in England. Her dad is single too. His name is Josiah, and he is the production design guy. Sarah seems mellow enough. She is my age but really petite. She is short and thin with long, curly blonde hair. She is quiet but laughs at all the jokes. She has a cool accent too.

I am the only one with red hair. Everyone comments on it, as usual. I don't mind. I used to hate my red hair, but now I am used to it. No one else has red hair, so I guess it is kinda cool. Aunt Rue will have her hands full juggling all these single men. I think she will be flustered.

My dad is right about the food. Nothing is too familiar on the menu, so I order fish and chips. The weird thing is that the fish and chips are served with peas. I hate peas. Who serves peas with anything these days? Jesse likes peas, so I give them to him. I don't even like having them on my plate. The fish pieces are really long. Instead of using cod for the fish, they use a fish called haddock. It is delicious though.

We talk about the adventures we want to have while we are here together. Everyone seems interested in pursuing the Loch Ness Monster. I am not telling dad, because he will put a stop to it. This could prove to be a very adventurous and mysterious trip. I am glad all these kids came, all except Judas and Goliath. I ask the others if they had met Judas and Goliath. They were all in agreement about trying to avoid him and his dog. I couldn't help but think of dad's words, though, when he had suggested that I not be so hard on Judas and his dog, but, instead, try and be nice. I feel a little guilty about bringing the subject up to the others. It just seems to me that dad doesn't really understand what I see and how devilish they both seem. I won't bring it up again, just in case dad does have a point. Maybe things will chill out between Goliath and ***Magic.*** Maybe they will become friends. It really seems doubtful though.

"So, tomorrow is everyone going to the festival?" Jesse asks.

"Yeah, I hear there is a sword sallower and lots of good snacks. There are supposed to be a lot of other performers too, like magicians," replies Jeremiah.

"Let's meet somewhere, so we can explore all this stuff together," suggests Jesse.

"That sounds brilliant," comments Sarah. "I really don't want to hang with my dad. I don't know what he will be doing at the festival, as far as the filming goes."

"My dad has already warned me to hook up with all of you, because he is going to be busy filming and needs to be focused. I thought I would be with my Aunt Rue, but, if I tell her I will be hangin' with you guys, she probably will go to the festival with my grandma." I remark.

"Let's hook her up with one of the single dads," laughs Jesse.

"Well, that is what my dad was hoping for on this trip. There are lots of single men." I reply. "My Aunt Rue will want me to hang with the other teenagers. She is really cool. She is a detective."

"Really? Does she hunt down serial killers?" Adam questions.

"She hunts down pretty much everything, but doesn't talk about it too much until it's all over," I reply. "My dad says there is a mall and another park by the mall with a clock made from flowers."

"Oh, I know where those are. The mall is called *The Prince's Mall* and the clock is right near there. We will have to go to both. The clock is brilliant." Sarah remarks.

"So where shall we meet? Finally, this is a chance to get away from all the adults we've been hanging around. Mom will be OK with this, don't you think?" Delilah addresses her sister, Anastasia.

"Well, if we tell her that everyone is older than us, especially Jesse, who is 16, she should let us go. After all, there are a whole group of us… mostly boys…to protect us." Anastasia laughs.

"My dad said that all of us kids were being taken by your limo and dropped off at the castle to watch the Tattoo performance tomorrow night. I'll talk with my dad to find out where the director wants him to be tomorrow for the festival on 'The Royal Mile'…uh, that's your mom, I guess," I say to the twins.

"I am sure she has it all planned out. She is a detail freak. I'll call you guys in the morning. We should all have each other's phone numbers anyway," Delilah responds.

We all exchange phone numbers as our parents get up to leave.

"Bye...see ya tomorrow," we all confirm as we depart.

"Well, it looks like you have got yourself quite a group of partners in crime," Aunt Rue teases.

"Yeah, actually...they are all really cool and into adventure," I reply.

"Don't tell your dad that," Aunt Rue warns.

"It looks like you have quite the selection of eligible bachelors." I tease Aunt Rue.

"Yeah, yeah, yeah," whines Aunt Rue. "We'll see."

Maybe I will make some friends after all.

♦ ♦ ♦ ♦ ♦ ♦

Chapter Fifteen
FRINGE FESTIVAL FEVER

Aunt Rue, Grandma, my dad, *Magic* and I all stand mesmerized, while gazing out our apartment windows to the narrow, cobblestone street below known as "The Royal Mile', which is crawling with action. The people are dressed in warm, black coats, black hats, and black umbrellas. It seems that most people here have dark hair, wear either dark casual clothes or nice suits like my dad wears sometimes. But many of the people are covered with tattoos and piercings. My dad calls it the 'gothic' look, which fits into this medieval place. I wonder if the 'gothic' look started in Scotland? There are practically no blonde haired adults, but lots of died black and red hair.

"It doesn't look like people here in Edinburgh are too into colors," comments Aunt Rue.

"Yeah, Noah was right about the whole 'gothic' atmosphere. It actually goes along with the medieval architecture though. It would look strange if everyone paraded around in polka dots or bright colors," Grandma responds.

"You're right. I definitely will have to invest in a dark coat to avoid suspicion," Aunt Rue confides.

"Suspicion!" Grandma exclaims, "Always the detective."

"Well I don't want to stick out like a sore thumb with my red coat. I prefer blending, especially in this environment. It looks pretty wild down there," responds Aunt Rue.

"Well, you should know," teases Grandma.

"So, did you hook up with any of the eligible men to experience the festival?" Dad questions Aunt Rue.

"I want to hang with mom," Aunt Rue responds.

"Oh, don't give up an exciting date in this gothic wonderland to hang with me," chimes in Grandma.

"Exciting date? I hardly think I would go right to exciting… Maybe interesting…but exciting? I am not going to hold my breath for any such occurrence," teases Aunt Rue.

"Check out all the people milling around down there. I can't wait to join the action and explore," I say.

"Where and when are you meeting your friends?" Dad asks with a concerned edge to his voice.

"I am not sure. They are supposed to contact me this morning and give me the details," I reply.

"Just be sure you all stick together. If you find yourself lost or not sure about something, call me. Use the walkie-talkie. Then I will know immediately you need something important. Don't be too anxious to seek out things you know nothing about. This looks like it could be a pretty sketchy crowd. I heard that this festival brings out all types from all over the world. It is that famous," Dad warns.

"Okay. I am sure we will all get the same instructions from parents. I can't imagine what would happen, except maybe we get lost in the midnight mist, locked in chains and fiercely thrown in a dungeon where death has no dominion!" I reply sarcastically.

"Very funny." Dad responds sarcastically as he grabs me around the neck with a headlock.

"Don't you two start wrestling in here. You're liable to break something," Grandma warns.

Magic is up and bouncing around, begging to get into the action.

"You are too much." Aunt Rue tells *Magic* as she squeezes her around the neck.

Surprisingly, the tall, dark and handsome Greek guy, Adino, contacts Aunt Rue to escort her around the festival. Grandma consents to go along.

"I will be the chaperone," teases Grandma.

"Oh, please. I can handle myself," says Aunt Rue defensively.

"That is what I am afraid of. I want to be sure you don't chase this hunky guy away," warns Grandma.

"Maybe you would like to date him instead?" Aunt Rue teases.

"Don't be wise. It will be an asset having a man escorting us around this very lively and daunting city," Grandma warns laughing.

My phone rings. As it turns out, we are going to meet down on the street in front of our apartment. The apartment building is really cool on the outside as well as the inside. It is on an alley off 'The Royal Mile.' Below our windows that look out on the street, there is a weathered, wooden sign with a picture of a pirate looking guy with a wig pointing down the skinny, cobblestone alley. The sign reads "Jolly Judge'. The alley leads to a dingy pub called the 'Jolly Judge' and the entrance to our apartment only few feet away from the pub. The pub is located down five stairs in a basement type room. There are white plastic tables and chairs sitting around on the street level of the pub on the cobblestone patio/alley.

The entrance to our apartment is a giant, royal blue door. There is a fob activation lock on the blue door that opens onto a spiral, stone staircase that leads up to our apartment. It is bizarre. Then right across from the big, blue door, in the cobblestone alley twenty feet from the pub, is a little, and I do mean little, bistro, where they serve coffee and pastries. It is also down five stairs into a basement type room. It is very convenient in the morning for snacks and coffee or hot chocolate. Last night, when we arrived back at the apartment after dinner, we could hardly access the big, blue door, because of the crowd of people swarming around the pub. What a city this is!

"Hey, Jesse… Adam." I call out as I approach the street.

"Hey there, Paul. This is wicked," exclaims Jesse.

"Isn't it? Is everyone here? Follow me and check out the big, blue door where we enter our apartment," I suggest excitedly.

"We are just missing Sarah. Oh, here she is," says Jesse.

"Sorry I'm late. The traffic was quite a challenge," Sarah replies. "It really turned cold today."

"OK, everyone is here. Let's go," I respond and take off leading the way to the big, blue door.

"Whoaaaa… How cool!" Everyone responds.

♦ ♦ ♦ ♦ ♦ ♦

♦ ♦ ♦ ♦ ♦ ♦

"I was a little suspicious about this big, blue door, but this is really cool back here. Oh look...there is a little bistro too. Check this out," Jesse continues commenting as he circles around the pub. "There are other apartments back here and the pub is in their parking lot."

Everyone is amused. We all make our way back to "The Royal Mile."

"Perfect name for this street," says Adam. We all agree, absorbed in the action going on everywhere.

"Look," cries Anastasia, "That woman is singing opera dressed like a Shakespearean actress. How cool! I love Shakespeare!"

Everywhere we look there is something going on. There are medieval plays, operas with multiple singers, musicians playing bagpipes and wearing Scottish kilts, accordions, violins, mimes with black and white faces dressed like court jesters, a guy dressed up with his face painted green and black like William Wallace from the movie *Brave Heart*, displays with birds on them like owls, falcons and other types of birds I've never seen before, and people handing out brochures for their plays, shops or attractions that are going on for the next two weeks. That is how long this Fringe Festival lasts. There are booths with snacks like cheese, breads, bangers—which are like sausages-ice cream and candy. I have never seen so much action, except at Disneyland.

"Let's head toward the park. My mom told me that there are some cool things going on there, like a sword swallower and musicians, and games," exclaims Adam.

"Yeah, mom was telling us about all that cool stuff this morning. She also gave us a pager in case we find ourselves in an emergency. It is like an instant alarm that she has attached to herself, so she can jump into action, if need be," says Anastasia.

"She sounds like my dad. I have a walkie-talkie type mode on my phone I need to activate, if we find ourselves lost or even worse, jailed." I laugh.

Magic shoves her way into the middle of us, and we pet her. We can't forget about her.

We start off down the street, and, as I glance down the alley, I see a dark object dart behind the pub. *Magic* must've seen it too, because she starts to pull me that way, and I won't let her. "Let's go," I say as I tug at her leash. *Could that have been Judas and Goliath?* I wonder. *Why would they be hanging around here? He must be spying on us. He and that dog are creepy,* I think to myself. I run to catch up with the others. I probably imagined it. I think he and his dog have me paranoid.

The park is amazing with games, young guys giving lessons on how to walk on stilts, more bright colored booths with food, musicians and, of course, the sword swallower. A pathway that winds through the park, a huge open area surrounded by all kinds of trees and the streets beyond. It is like a ball field, sectioned off for booths. The emerald, green grass is squishy from all the rain. No wonder there is this path. We have to veer off the path onto the squishy, muddy grass to check out the sword swallower. He is elevated up on a platform so we can all see. The crowd seems pretty quiet. I guess everyone must be nervous.

"Oooo… GROSS…," Anastasia, Delilah, and Sarah cry in unison as they spy the sword swallower.

The sword swallower looks really different than I expected. He is young and skinny with lots of tattoos. He has short blonde hair, which is unusual around here.

"I can't watch!" Sarah says. "What if he misses? Then we will watch him die."

"You have to watch," laughs Jesse as he stands next to her for encouragement.

"I have seen this before," says Jeremiah. "It seems to be a popular thing in Europe. I have never seen anyone miss…but I guess there is always a first time."

"Oh…you had to say that," laughs Delilah.

Anastasia turns away and says, "Tell me what happens… I can't watch."

Magic goes up to Anastasia and licks her hand and sits right next to her and nudges Sarah. Both girls glance down and pet *Magic.* She always knows when someone needs comfort.

"He's done. It's all the way in." I report. There he stands, with his eyes facing up to the heavens, his head thrown back, arms stretched out at his sides, mouth open and the handle of the sword protruding from his mouth.

"Yeah, Blimey, he did it!" Jesse exclaims.

Anastasia turns around, and Sarah uncovers her eyes to see the finished feat.

"Good grief, why would anyone want to do that?" Delilah exclaims.

"It's cool," replies Adam. "Who do you know that can swallow a sword and live to tell about it?"

"No one, thankfully," replies an indignant Delilah. "Only you would think it is cool."

"Wicked!" All of us boys chime in.

"I am just as worried about him pullin' it out," whines Sarah.

"Oh, here he goes." I say.

Magic is suddenly on the alert. She stands, her tail stiffens and her eyes start to glow. I am shocked at her response. I watch the sword swallower pull out the sword, while *Magic* stands at attention to him. *That is weird*, I think. *What is going on with her?* I wonder if anyone else notices. No one seems to. Why am I the only one who ever notices *Magic's* bizarre behavior?

"Wow that was amazing!" Jeremiah exclaims. "I wonder if he is going to do it again?"

"I hope not, but I am not going to stick around to watch it, if he does," Anastasia whines. "I believe once is enough for me."

"Lets get some ice cream and head to the Prince's mall and the other park," suggests Sarah.

Magic barks in agreement, all relaxed and out of her glowing mode. Everyone agrees to head to the mall.

No one appears to notic anything strange about *Magic*. I know I'm not imagining it. After that terrifying episode in the dungeon at the castle, I will never doubt *Magic's* special powers. What was she trying to do though? Did she see something scary or was she attunned to the sword swallower?

It starts to rain, for the first time today. It always seems to rain sometime during the day here. Luckily, we are all carrying umbrellas because, when it rains here…even if it is just for 10 minutes…it pours. We all walk hurriedly following Sarah, as she knows the way to the mall. That will be a good place to be when it's raining.

Magic stops, stands alert, and growls. I almost lose my balance with her abrupt stop. "*Magic*! What the heck!" I yell as I turn to see *her* glowing slightly. As I follow her gaze… I see them… Judas and Goliath… dispersing with the rest of the crowd. They are by some trees, and Goliath is tugging at Judas, Goliath's eyes blazing red, snarling…with crimson, glowing scary-looking teeth. He is zoned in on ***Magic***. I tug at ***Magic***… shove her with my leg and have to push and drag her away. She finally calms down. I turn to look and Judas and Goliath have disappeared.

"Hey, Paul. What's up? You wanna get soaked?" Jesse is laughing at me. The rest of the gang is standing under a tree watching me dance around with ***Magic***. I'm a little embarrassed and hope that maybe they saw the confrontation.

"Did you see them?" I ask hurriedly. "Judas and Goliath…you know…the weird boy and his dog?"

"We're trying to find cover and keep dry," says Adam.

Everyone laughs at me. I chuckle too. It is pretty funny. But… I know that there is no way I am gonna try and make friends with Judas and Goliath. They are evil, and ***Magic*** knows it. ***Magic*** must've been trying to protect that sword swallower guy. I think ***Magic*** is here to protect us. I know she is special, and, someday, maybe someone else will understand the things that I see.

"That is some dog!!!!" Sarah says as she slows to walk with me. I look at her and smile.

"Yeah, she is one of a kind." I reply.

◆ ◆ ◆ ◆ ◆ ◆

◆ ◆ ◆ ◆ ◆ ◆

◆ ◆ ◆ ◆ ◆ ◆

Chapter Sixteen
THE PRINCE'S MALL

The Prince's mall looks like any other mall. We could have been in any city or country. It's funny how that is. We also stop at the first department store in the world established in 1838. It is cool. It has 5 levels with a wooden staircase up the middle that reaches all the levels. It is called Jenners. Each level sells a different product. One level is a restaurant and bakery. They have all kinds of cakes shaped like jewelry, shoes, books, and cars and other stuff. It is kinda cool. We even get to take *Magic* in. There are lots of dogs around. People in Scotland take their dogs everywhere, even in restaurants.

"This is just like the malls at home," comments Delilah.

"I wonder who started the whole mall thing?" Anastasia replies.

"I don't know, and I don't care.!!" Sarah laughs. "They are brilliant!"

"All girls like malls," teases Adam.

Jesse responds laughing, "Where there are malls, there are girls, and where there are girls, that's where I want to be."

Everyone enjoys his comment.

"I don't believe it! There is Pizza Hut! Finally, some familiar food!!" I exclaim.

Magic starts dancing and barking.

"Your dog doesn't miss a thing." Sarah comments.

"I know. That's why I take her everywhere," I add.

"I am with you on that. I love having her with us," Sarah agrees.

"Does she like pizza?" Delilah teases.

"She likes almost anything!" I respond.

"Hey look. There is my Aunt Rue," I exclaim.

"It looks like she scored!" Jesse exclaims. "She is with that Greek guy, Adino. He is really cool."

"He must've not had to be with the film crew today," responds Anastasia. "Maybe they are all finished for the day." She checks her phone. "My mom said that, when they were all wrapped up for the day, she would call us and have the limo come get us…after we check out the flower clock at the park across the street."

"The clock is really cool. As long as you're here in Scotland, you may as well see famous attractions. There are always bagpipers hangin' around there. I like the sound of bagpipes…they are brilliant," comments Sarah.

"After the park, I will contact the driver. We can all fit in the limo. We should all go back to the castle…you know…where we had the original 'Meet and Greet' party." Anastasia says.

"That sounds awesome," replies Sarah.

"Good thinking, sis," responds Adam.

"Hi," I greet Aunt Rue and Grandma. "Check out your new black coat."

"Now I can blend. Did you guys meet Adino and Paul's Grandma?" Aunt Rue asks.

"Yes." Everyone responds.

"And, did you guys mange to stay out of trouble? Did you see that sword swallower? Wasn't that amazing?" Aunt Rue questions. "Grandma almost had a heart attack! She closed her eyes until he got it in and then wouldn't watch him take it out."

"That sounds familiar," Adam laughs as he shoves Anastasia.

"See, I am not the only one who thought it was creepy," chides Anastasia.

"Oh, and Paul and *Magic* had some kind of a standoff with that 'Goth guy', Judas, and his dog," informs Sarah.

"What?" Aunt Rue looks at me inquiring. "What is this?"

"Oh, it wasn't much. *Magic* saw Goliath and reacted," I reply.

"Not much!! Are you kidding? Paul and *Magic* were doing a dance on the grass, Paul almost biffing it in the muddy grass. It was pretty funny. I think *Magic* had the upper hand," Jesse teases.

"All right, all right, it wasn't that bad. ***Magic*** just caught sight of Goliath and they had a standoff like they did at the castle that night. Remember?" I respond.

"***Magic***, you little rascal. Always looking for action," Aunt Rue scolds as she pets ***Magic***.

"Sounds like a great gal to have around," replies Adino, smiling at ***Magic*** and Aunt Rue.

"Between Aunt Rue and ***Magic***, I am covered," I reply.

"Let's head to the park," says Jesse.

"See ya," I wave to Aunt Rue, Grandma and Adino.

◆ ◆ ◆ ◆ ◆ ◆

◆ ◆ ◆ ◆ ◆ ◆

◆ ◆ ◆ ◆ ◆ ◆ ◆

Chapter Seventeen
TERROR AT THE TATTOO

I really love the way we all have limos at our disposal. I forgot how cool that is. Ours is basic black with a T.V, bar, refrigerator, and a laptop. Colored lights ring the back ceiling and a panel in the back of the front seat moves up and down between the driver and us. The director's limo is longer and more elaborate than ours. It is snow white and has cushy, white leather seats, two TV's, a telephone, and amber lights circling the ceiling. There are two refrigerators and a huge wet bar and, of course, a laptop and ipad. There is also a panel, but it doesn't move up and down, as there is phone communication.

I haven't been on a trip in a while with my dad. I had forgotten about these limo perks. I remember thinking it was really cool the way my mom and I always met my dad by way of the limo, but I was too young to take advantage. She really liked it though. There were never any worries about transportation when we were traveling. I want to go on every trip from now on. So far, this has been a blast. It's so much more fun cuz I'm older and allowed to go off with the other teenagers. I am surprised the adults allow or trust us to venture off, but the driver always accompanies us, keeping an eye out, it seems. That's OK, since we are in a foreign country. It is actually reassuring to have an adult that knows the country to help us, if we need it.

The director's driver, Joseph, is pretty cool. He is about my dad's age, speaks with a thick Scottish accent, has a shaved head and wears casual clothes and a leather jacket. Our family rides around with James. He is nice too. He is younger than Joseph and looks like a body builder and wears a suit with a tattoo on his neck of a skeleton and has black slicked back hair. He kinda looks like a thug wearing a suit. He also has a very intense Scottish accent. They are really different drivers. My mom would have enjoyed this trip with me as a teenager and, of course, *Magic*.

It is daylight for a long time here. Consequently, the Tattoo performance starts about 8:30, and it is still just getting dusk. A major part of the performance is the light show on the castle. There are bleachers set up in a huge semi-circle around the outside of the castle, facing the entrance. It looks like a stadium. Hundreds of people of all ages and types roaming around trying to find their seats. It's drizzling with a misty fog hanging in the air and the crowds have their umbrellas up. It is curious to see a constant sea of umbrellas on and off all day long.

The air feels clean and crisp and cold. My face is cold and moist, but feels fresh. The drizzle gives the whole castle scene an atmosphere of mystery and intrigue. I feel like I have been transported back in time to the 16th century. It is amazing how this country has kept all the old medieval structures, which just make the whole place seem ancient and haunting.

"Right here...here. These are our seats," exclaims Jesse. "They are amazing seats. We are right in the middle, just elevated enough to see it all." We try and wipe off the moisture before we sit down.

"Brilliant!" Let *Magic* sit next to me." Sarah suggests as she looks pleadingly to me.

"Sure. *Magic* loves to be loved." I admit.

I am really glad that Sarah likes *Magic* so much because sometimes people are afraid of big dogs, and *Magic* **is** a big dog. She has huge paws and a big head. People often stop and ask me what kind of dog she is because she is so huge. She weighs about 125 pounds, and is perfectly proportioned. The other thing that makes her look so big is all her fur. Boy, when she gets alerted to something, she not only glows, but she gets extra fluffy. All the kids in our group seem to accept *Magic* as one of the gang.

"It should start any minute," Jeremiah reports.

"Does anyone want something to eat or drink?" asks Adam.

"Don't go. You might miss the beginning," responds Anastasia.

"What? We are going to listen to some bands and watch formations. It's not like I'm gonna miss the start of a play," says Adam laughing. Adam takes our orders and disappears.

I never knew watching bands do formations could be so cool. There are dancers and an amazing light show on the castle. It changes colors from red to blue to purple to orange, and images of crests of different families and school emblems that are being represented by the bands are projected on the castle. There are a lot of bagpipes involved. There are bands from all over the world represented here. I think that is what brings all the people from everywhere to this Festival, like my dad was saying. There are so many people in the bands and, of course, the families of the bands and dancers and festival performers. This is quite a happening here in Scotland every August. No wonder Rachel, my dad's boss, wanted to come and film at this time. This is great advertisement for tourism. The only thing is that it is sooooo cold. All of us are wearing gloves, scarves and warm coats and beanies.

"Oh no. I dropped my phone. My dad will kill me!" I exclaim.

"Quick, go down those stairs, hop under the bleachers and fetch it before someone steals it!" Sarah suggests.

"OK, watch *Magic.*" I reply.

"Sure. Just hurry," Sarah says.

I crawl over everyone seated in our row and hop down the stairs leading under the bleachers. "Great. It's super dark down here...let me find where we are sitting." I whisper to myself.

I get under where I think it might have fallen and drop to my hands and knees. It is like cobblestone, so at least I may have a chance...if it didn't break. *It sure is spooky down here. Boy...they really turn off all the lights, and the bands sound far away.* As I feel around... I hear a strange noise. It sounds really eerie...like a high-pitched whine. I think maybe it is a type of bagpipe. My hand touches something small and hard. Yeah... it's my phone. Relieved... I turn and sit down...only to be face to face with Goliath glowering above me...fiery red eyes piercing the darkness. His mocking smile, curls up to reveal glowing razor sharp red teeth... glistening from the dark depths. My phone in hand, I timidly click a picture. Goliath rears up from the flash...lunging forward as I make a quick surge to escape his massive body.

All I could think of is a hideous death rising before me...being ripped apart by this black beast...those vicious teeth. Suddenly there is a blinding flash of lightening... In a fleeting instant, I am being propelled away...while witnessing the savage attack of my massive, electrified *Magic*...hurling Goliath into the dark, imposing, thick hedges that edge the bleachers. There is a blood curdling scream...the sound I heard when I was alone in the dungeon of the Edinburgh castle... *Magic* surges forward, swift-footedly, colliding with the monstrous chest of Goliath... her massive strength overpowering his existence. No one was around to witness this madness that was going to try and kill **Magic...**

I pray silently, hoping against all odds that God or an angel would be here...especially this time...to give *Magic* the strength to prevail. Glancing around, I can't help but wonder where Judas is.

I scream frantically...but pathetically...considering what was happening before my eyes. "*Magic*, let it go, let it go"...as if she could hear me. I couldn't bear the thought of *Magic* dying at the wrath of this roaring fiend.

They tear through the hedge in a massive fiery ball...leaves and branches flying everywhere. Some security guy comes running up. "Blimie! What the heck is going on here?"

The savage screaming suddenly fades and everything seems still. The guy yells as he sees me creeping out from under the bleachers, "What was that noise and commotion?"

"I have no idea," I say. "I was under the bleachers looking for my phone I dropped. See, here it is. It sounded like someone was going to die though."

Magic comes trotting out from around one of the check points set up for tickets down the walk, looking as if nothing happened. *"Magic!"* I scream. She comes up and puts her paws on me and literally hugs me around the waist. There is blood dripping from her mouth onto her fur. I quickly inspect her mouth for a cut, while the security guy comes closer.

"Well, she looks calm enough. I wonder what that hideous sound was?" The guy exclaims. "Is she OK? Are you OK?"

"Yeah...uh...she seems to be fine. I don't think she was involved with whatever that was...but... I...um...am getting out of here. I don't want to know…what all that was." I reply as I peer up the hill towards where the security guy had appeared.

"I am with you. Something sure ripped through these hedges." The guy says as he turns to walk up the hill hurriedly.

Ahead of him, lurking in the shadows of the light from another checkpoint booth, I spy two dark figures. One is definitely a dog. They swiftly disappear into the shrubs, as the security guy heads up the hill. I inspect *Magic* again for blood and cuts, but the blood has disappeared completely. *Magic* seems fine…happy…even.

"Paul!" Sarah exclaims as she startles me. "There you two are. The weirdest thing happened when you were looking for your phone, and I was petting *Magic*. She got really warm and I could swear she started to glow… like sparkly neon gold. Then she tore away from me…forced herself under the bleachers…leaving me holding her lease. I didn't think anything could fit through that space. Have you ever seen her do anything like that?"

"Yeah… I can't believe you saw the sparkles. No one ever believes me when I say she sparkles and glows sometimes," I reply. "Did the others notice?"

"I don't think so. Everyone was watching the performance. Come on; let's go back up. It is dodgy and creepy down here." Sarah says timidly.

"Did you hear anything?" I ask Sarah.

"Just the bands playing. Why? What did I miss?" Sarah questions.

"Let's go." I attach *Magic* to the leash that Sarah has brought and grab Sarah by the arm. I lead them up the bleachers, looking around in search of anything suspicious. I wonder where they disappeared?

"We need to chat and sort this out." Sarah says as we settle into the bleachers to watch the rest of the show.

I check my phone to see the picture I snapped…there were only two red, glowing ovals on a dark screen

◆ ◆ ◆ ◆ ◆ ◆

Chapter Eighteen
THE ROAD TO INVERNES

We will be traveling into the highlands, or mountains of Scotland on the next leg of our journey. The trip will be three hours. It won't be too bad because we get to ride in a limo. All the parents want their own kids with them, since we are traveling in another country. The director is very strict about that. I am surprised we were allowed to go back to Adam's and the twins' castle after the mall yesterday and then on to the Tattoo performance, which turned out to be terrifying.

"Make sure you get all your belongings." Dad warns. "Once we are outa here, there is no turning back."

"You make it sound like we are going on a doomed adventure," teases Grandma while she makes breakfast.

"Well, we are in a foreign country, so it is difficult to retrace steps or even contact anyone. We would have to go through the production company to retrieve anything left behind. It will be a hassle that I would like to avoid, so just make sure you have your stuff," Dad replies.

"Where are we staying once we get there?" I ask, lounging with **Magic** on the sofa as we look out the window for one last moment of the 'Fringe Festival. "I am sure gonna miss this city. I wish we were staying longer."

"We will be making a few stops along the way, filming various places. We will be mostly focused on the Urquhart Castle, which sits beside Lock Ness…the famous lake where your long lost friend, the Lock Ness Monster… Nessie…supposedly lives. These places are in the highlands or mountain areas of Scotland. We will be going to the Isle of Sky first, which is one of many islands that connect with the Atlantic Ocean. The islands are supposed to be beautiful with very little population and many emerald green, mossy hills with water flowing down them in random places and sheep grazing in clusters everywhere." Dad replies.

"This is a beautiful country," Aunt Rue exclaims. "I will say that for it. The medieval architecture just enhances the beauty and history of this whole adventure. This is really one of my favorite places that I have visited!"

"I agree. I wish Rebecah could have been here. She was a fiend for medieval history and lush scenery. Your mom would have loved this trip, Paul. She would have also been excited to try and encounter 'Nessie' as well," teases Grandma.

We all are silent, remembering my mom in our own way. We all have a special place in our hearts for her. She always made everything more fun. We all miss her.

"As I mentioned to you before…the Urquhart castle, mostly ruins, is famous and dates back from the 13th century to the 16th century. There are a lot of nooks and crannies to explore. The castle played a role in the Wars of Scottish Independence in the 14th century Because of this, it came to be regarded as a 'royal castle'. It is one of the largest castles in the Scotland area. It even had a drawbridge. The castle is quite close to the water level. There was a dry moat around the castle that would defend the landward approach of enemies.

I am really anxious to see this famous place with such an historical castle and the famous Loch Ness Monster, which your mom was also obsessed with," Dad says as he smiles and looks at me. We all agree with that, especially me. Mom and I always shared our Loch Ness Monster fantasies with each other.

I am anxious to reunite with all my new friends. This is the best trip ever. I think this group of kids are perfect, even the girls. They are different than other girls I know. Most girls I know are mean and act stupid. The girls on this trip are really cool. Maybe it is because they are older than me or from other places. I am really nervous about what Sarah said to me…though…about needing to talk. I know she noticed *Magic's* fur glowing and her feeling extra warm. I wonder what she wants to talk about.

The ride is just like my dad said it would be...amazing. There is water flowing everywhere down the tall, emerald green mountains. Most of the mountains and hills look like they are covered with moss and sheep graze on the slopes. There are mountains that are purple because they are covered with heather, an abundant flower in Scotland. Thistle, the national flower is everywhere as well. It's purple as well. My dad says the heather is important to the sheep because it does not die in the snow. The sheep can easily see it to eat. The thistle is really thorny, so the Scots would plant it around their homes and castles, so intruders would get stuck in it. We travel through little villages with very narrow streets. Two cars can hardly pass each other.

We stop at a picnic area out in the middle of the country, where there is a little snack shop. We buy some snacks and head out to the back where there are some picnic benches. After we eat, we take a hike down a winding trail lined with ferns and towering trees. It is so cool...like a rain forest. Moss is covering all the surfaces. Everything is green and misty... It is awesome... Great for an adventure...probably like the 'Garden of Eden'. *Magic* sniffs around at everything. We take some family pictures and enjoy nature. It is really quiet and pretty. I am sure we are all thinking about how much my mom would've loved this pretty place. If only she could've known *Magic.*

We have to drive across a huge bridge called the Skye Bridge to get to the islands. We go to the Isle of Skye, which is the largest of the islands. The coastline of Skye is a series of peninsulas and bays radiating out from a center, which are mostly hills. It is a very irregular coastline and is sixty miles long. The main industries are tourism, agriculture, fishing and whiskey distilling. That is why we are here to film. It is a very famous island because of its beauty. I guess they film a lot of movies here, and it is mentioned in poems and books. Sheep graze everywhere on the rolling green hills.

We are starting to converge with the other limos. I want to see the whiskey distilling place and the fishing villages. It is really cool how there will be a random red, old-fashioned phone booth out in the middle of nowhere. I wonder if we will be allowed to explore. The tide pools look awesome. My dad says to watch for golden eagles, red deer and, of course, sheep.

I am pretty sure that **Magic** is going to have fun running on the shoreline chasing birds. The weather today is really perfect. There are some fluffy white clouds, light winds, and it is about sixty degrees. It is the most perfect weather day we have seen. I guess the weather is like this most of the time on this island.

"Hey, make sure **Magic** doesn't get all wet and dirty." Dad calls to me as **Magic** and I head toward the water. "I don't want to mess up the limo, since we have to drive around in it for several more days."

"Really? Are you kidding me?" I shout back as I turn towards my dad.

"You want to answer to the Limo Company?" Dad responds as he catches up to me quickly.

"Don't we have a towel or something we could use for her to lay on or clean her up?" I plead.

Just then we hear a call. "Hey, Mr. Wonder." It is the limo driver, James, calling to us. He is holding up a huge beach towel smiling. My dad and I look at each other and do a 'high five'.

Magic, of course is already running down the beach.

◆ ◆ ◆ ◆ ◆ ◆ ◆

Chapter Nineteen
URQUHURT RUINS

The Isle of Skye is a blast. We kids get to explore all the tide pools and whiskey factory. The adults even let us have a shot of whiskey. The people who run the whiskey factory give everyone free samples. It tastes awful. All of us kids are coughing. The adults like it. This factory, if that is what you could call it, is a small wooden building out in the middle of nowhere. It is off a dirt road up from a boat dock where fishermen kept their fishing gear. Everything is quaint and casual on Sky. There are houses here and there along the water, and sheep are grazing everywhere.

Driving along Loch Ness is incredible. *Loch* means "lake" in Gaelic, which is a language some people in Scotland speak. They are actually starting to teach Gaelic in the schools again. The lake is huge. My dad says it is the largest volume of fresh water in Great Britain. It is eight hundred feet deep and is twenty-three miles long. My dad says that accounts of an aquatic beast living in the lake date back to AD 500. There are even accounts of the beast killing people. From the size of this lake, I can imagine that anything could be living in there.

We arrive at the Urquhurt castle late afternoon, after filming on the Isle of Skye most of the day. The Urquhurt castle sits on Loch Ness, just like my dad said. It is very spooky looking. The lake and sky look dark gray. The castle sets out by the water and is also dark gray and has a tall, round tower. We stand on the street and look out over a lush, emerald green, grassy field between the castle and us. The grass looks like velvet. It is perfectly groomed. There is a big contrast between the shocks of color on the landscape and the general grayness everywhere else, The hills are shades of green and purple and the flowers are brilliant blue, red, yellow and pink, but the buildings, the water and the sky are colorless. Near the castle, slightly around the cove, is a boat dock that takes tourists out on the lake.

We are going to stay at a very large, castle-like 'Bed and Breakfast' near the Urquhurt castle. Several of these places are reserved for the crew. There aren't many motels or hotels. We either rent an apartment or stay at a 'Bed and Breakfast'. Ours is a three-story building across from the lake. The lake looks more like a river running through the middle of town with small bridges connecting the two side. There are neighborhoods around this area. We are staying in a town called Inverness. That is where Lock Ness is located. It is a huge lake but then tapers into a river. The Urquhurt castle is on a wider part of the river about one mile from our 'Bed and Breakfast.'

A Scottish man who owns the Bed and Breakfast greets us. His name is Raynor, which means a strong warrior, he volunteers. People are really into names and clans in Scotland. He shows us to our rooms, two flights up. Of course, there are no elevators, so we have to lug our bags up two flights of stairs.

"Hey Paul, there is someone here to see you," Dad calls to me in my room. I'm trying to unpack and get settled, because we are going to be here for a couple of days.

"Lover boy," Aunt Rue teases as she walks past me and tussles my hair.

"What?" I whine to her.

"Get out there, lover boy," she teases again.

I walk out into the common area and there is Sarah.

"Hi Paul," she says. "Our flat is down the hall a bit. I think Jesse and Jeremiah are here as well. I am not sure where everyone else is, but I just wanted to let you know who all was here at this Bed and Breakfast, Weren't those stairs beastly? That bloke running the place was pretty cheeky about it as well when I commented on no elevators."

"Oh, hey thanks for stopping by. Come in and check out the place. It's really cool. How's your place?" I ask.

"It is not as large as this one, but that is probably because it is just my dad and me," Sarah replies.

"I was thinking about going across the street and checking out the lake. Do you and *Magic* want to go with me?" Sarah asks. "I don't want to get eaten by the lake monster, and I really wanted to chat with you about *Magic*."

"Actually, that is a great plan, because my dad and aunt are going to meet the others at the pub down the street. They want to 'soak up the local color' as my dad always puts it," I reply.

"I would really fancy a look at that lake. It is brilliant… You know, with all the legends. Should we invite Jesse and Jeremiah?" She asks.

"Well, if you want to talk about *Magic*, we better not invite anyone else, because *Magic* is special, and, when I speak of her being extraordinary…people think I am nuts. Even my dad and aunt think I imagine stuff. I can't imagine Jesse and Jeremiah not wanting to explore the lake as well as my Aunt Rue. I imagine we will run into people whether we want to or not." I reply.

"Okay then… I will go get my jumper and bonnet. It will probably be cold. I will meet you out front then. See ya," Sarah calls as she leaves the room. "By the way. Be sure and grab some biscuits on the way out. They serve them in the morning and afternoon."

"Hey *Magic*. You wanna go for a walk?" I ask. Of course those words always send *Magic* into frenzy.

"Hey Dad, Sarah and I and maybe Jesse and Jeremiah are going to go check out the lake," I call out.

"Whoaaa, wait a minute. It is going to be dark in a while. Where are you going? I don't want to have to worry all night about you guys getting into some kind of trouble," Dad replies.

"Always trouble. Do you really think I am that stupid? I know we are in another country. I am in no hurry to have something awful happen… we are just going across the street to check out the lake and let *Magic* get some exercise," I reply somewhat irritated.

"Wow, aren't we testy? It is a good thing your grandma didn't hear you speak that way to me," Dad replies kinda hurt.

"I'm sorry, Dad. I understand where you are coming from. Believe me, if I get suspicious or nervous about anything, I will definitely come find you. Honest. I want this to be a great trip too. I just don't want you to spend all your time worrying about me, when you should be enjoying yourself too," I respond.

"I get it. I know you are a teenager, and I need to be a little looser on the reigns. You know, at home, I am very open to you and your friends going to the beach and store and movies on your own. I trust you. I just get a little nervous in a foreign country. Besides, I don't want you to get eaten by Nessie," Dad responds laughing.

"Yeah, yeah," I say as I head out the door. "Where are you going to be?"

"Ruthie and I are meeting the others at the pub about a block down the street," Dad offers.

"Well, have fun. How long are you going to be out?" I ask.

"Now who is being a busy body?" Dad retorts laughing.

"Oh, sorry, uh…uh, I just meant when should I send out the search party, if you don't return. Watch out for Nessie!" I tease.

"Oh, yeah. I am sure we will be watching over our shoulders all night. We will be home early, because we have to get an early start in the morning," Dad replies.

"OK then. Bye… Have fun," I say as I go out the door.

◆ ◆ ◆ ◆ ◆ ◆

Chapter Twenty
DISCOVERY AT LOCH NESS

"Hey Sarah," I call.

"Hi. I thought you changed your mind. I grabbed some biscuits, did you?" Sarah asks.

"Oh, uh…no. My dad was giving me the third degree about my activities tonight, and I forgot about the…biscuits? Those look like cookies to me," I say as I look at the cookie Sarah is offering me.

"Oh, sorry. We call cookies biscuits in England," She laughs. "But anyway, I grabbed a few for our walk. I thought *Magic* might like one too."

"Hey *Magic*, we have treats." I pet her head. She is raring to go as she pulls on the leash.

"Did you bring any gear to fight off the monster?" Sarah laughs.

"Nah. I never worry too much with *Magic* around. She is pretty protective. Are you up for walking a ways?" I inquire.

"Well, what did you have in mind? I didn't bring a backpack, and I don't think these biscuits will sustain us for long," Sarah teases.

"Funny. No, really. I want to walk down to the castle. We might never have another chance at night. I think it is now or never. I definitely want to explore this shoreline at night. I can't come all the way to Scotland and not delve into trying to get a glimpse of Nessy. My mom would definitely be disappointed in me," I reply.

"Why didn't your mom come on this trip? Does she not fancy traveling?" Sarah asks as they walk along the path next to the lake.

"Oh… I guess you wouldn't know. My mom died a few years back. She died of cancer," I respond. "She was a fiend about the Loch Ness monster. She and I always read everything we could on 'Nessy'."

Sarah stops in her tracks. "I'm sorry. That is really strange because my mum died too. She died in childbirth. My baby brother and her both died. That is why it is just my dad and I," Sarah says very sadly.

"That is strange," I comment. "I mean, it is strange that we both lost our moms. I have never met anyone who lost his or her mom so tragically as us. I am sorry for your loss and that you never knew her. Do you know anyone else who lost a parent?"

"No. I have never been able to share with anyone how horrible it is to lose one's mum, of all people," Sarah responds.

"Well, maybe you and I losing our moms are why we seem to have a similar connection to *Magic.* I know that sounds insane…but, when you asked me about *Magic* and her fur glowing… I was surprised. Everyone always makes fun of me, when I ask them if they saw her eyes sparkle or her fur glow," I say excitedly. "This way. Let's walk by the shore of the lake." "Really…though…what did you want to know about *Magic?*"

As we are walking, I notice that the day is fading from dreary to dusk. Shadows are becoming darker as the lake takes on an ominous hue. The opposite shore is shrouded in a feathery mist. *This is a perfect atmosphere for exploring Lock Ness,* I thought to myself.

"Well…that night at the Tattoo performance, after you took off to go get your phone… *Magic* got really tense." Sarah says. "I was petting her and I could feel her body…like…swell and get warm. I inspected her fur as I thought the light show was making her sparkle…but nothing else was glowing or sparkling. She wouldn't take her eyes off you. Then she exploded through those bleachers under our seat. I don't even know how she fit through the tiny space. The people around me laughed at the whole thing…but I was scared. I didn't know what to do. All I know is that *Magic* got warm and sparkly and huge and disappeared under the bleachers. I know it sounds barking mad…but that is why I have been anxious to meet with you and chat about your amazing dog and what I saw," Sarah relays to me excitedly.

Finally… I thought…someone who has seen Magic transform into an amazing creature. I didn't know what to say. I stopped and looked at Sarah and Magic. I laughed and petted *Magic.* "You wouldn't believe what

Magic is capable of. She has saved my life many times. She appeared out of nowhere when she was a puppy, and we kept her. She has always been a mystery. Everyone knows she is special, even if they haven't been able to see what I see. I know now that her sparkling…glowing…swelling up…is not my imagination. Thank you for telling me about this. I was beginning to think that maybe I am crazy," I tell Sarah.

"Tell me about a time when she saved your life," Sarah demands.

"Well…she saved my life under the bleachers at that Tattoo performance. There is a lot you don't know about things that have happened since we arrived in Scotland," I respond.

Suddenly, I can sense a thick, shadowy gloom…hanging hauntingly…engulfing us as our steps noiselessly found our way through the moist grass. The mist had traveled around the bend and was swirling around our ankles, making it seem like we were walking on clouds.

"Wait." I whisper as I grasp Sarah's arm. She looks at me with concern. "Do you feel anything weird? I mean…like do you sense a dread in the air?"

"You're scaring me." Sarah whispers.

"Over there," I point. "Did you see that movement?"

"Uh…maybe…we should…run up the bank onto the street," She stammers.

"Hold on…we have *Magic*. Let's investigate," I suggest as I gently push Sarah behind me. "Follow me." *Magic*…already alerted…is pulling me. I let the leash go, so she can run ahead.

"Whooaa, *Magic*," someone exclaims from ahead of Sarah and me.

Suddenly, Jesse and Jeremiah appear with *Magic*. "What are you trying to do…scare the pants off us?" Jesse exclaims.

"Oh…it's you guys." I chuckle.

"We heard some sounds in those bushes, and we were trying to decide whether we should investigate or not…but it's just *Magic*." Jeremiah replies. "This place is creepy with all this mist and fog. Then we heard some rustling in the bushes. I feel like we are in a horror film.

"I saw something lurking around those bushes too. That's why I let *Magic* go ahead. Come on…let's check it out," I insist as I walk toward a clump of bushes up the hill a little.

"Are you sure it is important?" Sarah whines.

"You can stay here on the path...if you want. Lets go guys. ...Come on *Magic*." I say.

"No...uh...that's ok. I don't want to stay here being spooked by myself. I'll come along. Let me walk in the middle though... Let *Magic* go ahead," Sarah begs.

"Someone is scared," teases Jeremiah. Sarah shoots him a glaring look.

"Oh, belt up, and let's go before I lose my nerve all together," warns Sarah. "Besides, you just said yourself that you thought it was creepy around here.

As we turn to go...we hear a gurgling sound and a giant, swirling wave erupts from the misty, shadowed lake and engulfs all of us...knocks us off our feet. We sputter and try to scurry up the embankment. I turn and look for *Magic*. There she is...standing perfectly dry at the edge of the foreboding, tumultuous lake. Before we can react, we hear an unearthly, demonic ear piercing scream...exploding from up the path. We freeze...and look at each other. *Magic* alerts, swelling up...her tail stiff...her fur glowing...as she takes off and bursts forth through the bushes up ahead and out of sight.

"MAGIC!!!" we all scream.

"Let's go." I call frantically.

I round the slippery bend along the lake and witness the aftermath of a vicious attack of some hideous entity from the lake. Disappearing back into the rippling depths of the menacing lake is the likes of some creature I never imagined... I see an enormous, black, spiky, pointed tail. It is curled into the air about twenty feet up...like a giant, spiked crocodile tail. It slithers back into the water, spiraling out of sight.

On the banks stands *Magic*...in all her **GLORY**...puffed up... unrecognizable. Next to her is a bloody mound. There is blood everywhere with chucks of something furry scattered about. Facing off...on the other side of the bloody mound from *Magic*...is an enraged, engorged, fiery, red-eyed Goliath. He has horns the size of a bull...his demonic teeth are razor sharp and crimson red...he looks ready to attack. The atmosphere is charged with an incomprehensible feeling of evil.

I scream to *Magic*, "No... *Magic*...come here."

Out of the menacing shadows appears Judas. I straighten up and scream at him... "Call your devil dog off." I gingerly approach *Magic* and touch her back as Judas approaches Goliath. He grabs Goliath's collar and orders him to come away.

Jeremiah and Jesse comfort Sarah who is crying, as **Magic** and Goliath deflate and evolve back into themselves. Judas and I look at each other. I think we are both scared. I back off with **Magic** in tow...still facing the two devil inspired entities. I am so scared I can't speak... No one can.

Judas finally speaks. "This is not how it looks. When Goliath and I arrived here, a hideous creature from the lake was attacking this sheep... Goliath got into the mix."

"WHAT THE HECK IS HAPPENING HERE?!!!!" yells Aunt Rue as her and Adino come running up. "What was that deafening scream?"

We are all still speechless, Sarah crying and Jesse and Jeremiah still comforting her with their arms around her...protection mode.

Judas shouts, "Let's get outta here, before we get blamed for this!" He and Goliath turn and jog off down the path towards the castle.

"WHOA, NOT SO FAST!" Aunt Rue chases after him yelling.

"Wait Ruthie, come back!" Adino calls as he runs towards her. "I don't think we need to mess with him. We will contact the authorities." Aunt Rue stops and listens...unbelievably. She must be afraid too because Aunt Rue never listens. She is experienced with crime...though...so she knows what to do. They walk back. Aunt rue comes up to me and hugs **Magic** and me. She walks to Sarah and the others, and puts her arm around Sarah.

"Are you OK Sarah? What in heaven's name happened here...and why is everyone wet...except **Magic**? I turn my back on you guys for one evening, and look what happens. Wait 'til your dad gets wind of this. He is gonna hit the roof!" Aunt Rue exclaims.

"Please Aunt Rue. Do we have to tell him? Can't we just take care of this ourselves or think of something to tell him?" I plead. "He'll never let me go off by myself again."

"This is serious, Paul. You kids could've been lying here instead of whatever this bloody thing is." Aunt Rue says with concern in her voice. "Who's idea was it to come down by this lake at night?"

"Yes, she is right. This is something for the authorities. Killing animals is serious business around here." Adino responds as he stoops to inspect the bloody mound. Aunt Rue follows his lead and goes to the bits of fur and blood scattered about. "I think it's a sheep. It is hard to tell, it is so mutilated," comments Adino.

"Oh yuk." Exclaims Sarah. "How beastly!! Do you think that gigantic, red eyed, horned black beast...of that boy in black...did this?"

"Horned black beast!" Jesse exclaims. "All I saw was a enormous black dog and a creepy looking gothic boy."

"WHAT? Are you kidding me? You didn't see that dogs huge teeth and horns?" Sarah questions.

"That wave from the lake must've made you daft or got in your eyes. Maybe you are in shock." Jesse says concerned as he walks to her to see if she is OK.

I grab Sarah's arm and look at her. "I told you." I whisper.

"Really? You too? What wave? Am I missing something here? Is that why you are all wet? Were you in the lake?...God forbid!" Aunt Rue is startled as she looks from Sarah to me.

We both just clam up and look at her.

"Well I am just happy all of you are fine. What do you think happened?" Aunt Rue questions, as Adino walks up and puts his arm around her. I look at her and roll my eyes and chuckle. "Never mind with the eyes, Paul. Let's stay focused. Which one of you had the bright idea of exploring the shores of this haunted lake? You still haven't come up with an answer, and what the heck went on here, and why are you all wet?"

"Sarah and I decided to explore the lake with **Magic**, of course, while we had a chance, since you had other engagements." I smirk as I address Aunt Rue. "What, may I ask, were you doing down here...at night...by yourselves...?

"Never mind what I am doing here. I am an adult and an experienced detective. Adino wanted to explore the castle and lake, and I came along to protect him." Aunt Rue retorts.

"Oh, yeah right." I say as we all chuckle.

"What about you boys and why is everyone wet and shivering?" Aunt Rue repeats as she interrogates Jesse and Jeremiah.

"We were just tired of sitting on the bus all day and didn't want to stay in the room...and all the adults were going to the pub...which we are not allowed in...so here we are," replies Jesse.

"Well the most important thing is...what did you see and what happened and, again, why is everyone wet?" Aunt Rue questions impatiently in her detective mode.

"We were just walking along the path...me and Jeremiah here... and we ran into *Magic.* So we knew Paul must be nearby; and then, he and Sarah appeared...around the bend in the path," reports Jesse.

"Sarah and I were strolling along the path when we felt a shadowy, gloomy type feeling surrounding us" I say. "I noticed some movement in the bushes up ahead from us and sent *Magic* to investigate. That's when we ran into Jesse and Jeremiah. We all decided to investigate my suspicions together...when there was this tornado like enormous wave that grew out of the lake and engulfed us...knocking us over and smashing us against the hillside." I relay.

"We had almost recovered," I continued," when we heard this demonic, ear piercing scream...the one you two heard...and we ran toward where we thought it was coming from, and we saw this gigantic... black...horned tail twenty feet in the air swirl and go down with a noiseless retreat into the lake."

"It was an awesome monster!" Jeremiah exclaims. "Huge tail!"

"I have heard enough here. Let's get out of here, before that monster resurfaces and attacks us. Thank the Lord an angel was watching out for you guys. You may not be so lucky next time," exclaims Aunt Rue." Oh look... I think that is the sheep's brains. Don't step on it. Watch where you are going! This is a mess. It is like a sheep exploded."

We all head up the hill toward the street.

"Can we explore the castle, since we're here?" I ask excitedly. Everyone groans.

"You are barking mad!" Jesse exclaims.

◆ ◆ ◆ ◆ ◆ ◆

Chapter Twenty-One
CONFESSIONS

"I knew something like this was going to happen!" Dad exclaims.

"Nothing really happened to us… We are all fine. It's…well…the poor sheep is what got mangled. But…don't you see…there is a 'Nessy'. We saw it…and the sheep is proof!" I exclaim back to dad.

"Nessy, indeed. That's all we need is to have a run in with an ancient monster," Dad retorts. "And what were you doing down by the lake at night? And why are you all wet?"

"OK, everyone relax. Paul is right. No one got hurt, save the poor sheep… I think that is what it was. What about Judas and his dog, Goliath?" Aunt Rue questions, "Couldn't that big black beast have torn the sheep apart?"

"We saw the humongous, spiked tail of the monster retreat back into the water!! Are you kidding me? There can be no question about what we saw!!" I respond excitedly.

"You should've seen it!" Jeremiah cries.

"It was unbelievable!" Jesse admits.

"It was definitely a weird, beastly creature!" Sarah agrees.

By now the rest of the people in the pub were gathering around us to hear our accounts. Everyone starts to talk at once.

"Take us there!" A man in the pub shouts.

"Yeah…we want to see this sheep that was mangled by the monster. This won't be the first time!" yells another man in the pub.

"Oh, for the love of Pete…let's just get the authorities to handle this," responds dad.

"I saw the scene and the sheep. I am a detective, and I am qualified to make a judgment, and it was a torn up sheep. We need to get someone to come clean up the mess," pleads Aunt Rue.

"Well, that is true...but we need to contact the authorities in Inverness. Animal killing is a serious business around here," advises the pub owner. "Oh, good you're here." The pub owner says to an arriving policeman.

"What's all the fuss about?" The officer questions the owner.

"There has been another mutilation down by the lake. These kids say they saw some beastly creature at the lake and a sheep that is no longer. I think we need to sort this out. Blimey...this is big news around here. There hasn't been a citing of 'ol Nessy for years," says the pub owner. "This is great advertisement for my pub!"

'Let's not get ahead of ourselves now...it may have been a big fish the kids saw...you know how it is with the shadows...the mist...they can play tricks on your eyes," replies the officer.

"Well, you can call it what you want to... I've never seen a fish with a gigantic, spiked tail like we saw!" Jeremiah exclaims. "Go check it out for yourself. That sheep was torn to pieces by something other than a big dog or a giant fish or shadows...as you say!"

"OK, OK, let's go have a look... You kids stay here," responds the officer.

"Adino and I are coming along," Aunt Rue informs him.

"I better go too," Dad says. "You kids stay here, and try to stay out of trouble...will ya?"

"I'll stay with them and make sure they keep under wraps, and get them warm," replies Sarah's dad. "How about something to eat or drink? Come here and sit by the fire"

I wonder what they think they are going to find? We already know what happened. The monster, Nessy, tore the sheep to shreds, and Judas and Goliath and all of us were lucky not to be next. There is a monster, and it's on the loose.

Magic whines… I bend down and hug her, thanking God she wasn't torn up.

◆ ◆ ◆ ◆ ◆ ◆

Chapter Twenty-Two
THE STREETS OF INVERNESS

The 'Bed and Breakfast' is really cool. The guy, Raynor, who owns it, make us a great breakfast. There are plenty of tables in the dining room on the first floor. All the tables have white tablecloths and colorful flowers on them. The buffet is amazing with fruit, meats, pastries, juices, coffee, hot chocolate, and a cook makes us any type of eggs we want. It is really delicious. The cook even gives *Magic* a hearty snack.

"Ok...today I want our activities to be a little less dramatic. The director will be sorry she encouraged us to bring our kids. I want to be able to bring you on other trips...so can you cool your investigative adventures for one afternoon?" Dad asks Aunt Rue and me.

"Oh, please. I simply happened upon the whole incident...luckily... so I could bring the kids and the dog...of course...to you," replies Aunt Rue.

"Well...what I am wondering is what in the world YOU were doing wandering around down by the lake with Adino...of all people?" Dad questions.

"If it was any of your business I might tell you...but it isn't...and besides the pub was stuffy, and we wanted to take a look at Loch Ness at night. It was eerie... I have to admit. We were ready to head back when we heard the scream," volunteers Aunt Rue.

"There was a scream? No one mentioned a scream. Who screamed? Is there something you aren't telling me?" Dad questions.

"Oops... I guess I did neglect mentioning the scream. It all happened so fast...and there was the mutilated sheep...and..." replies Aunt Rue.

"Don't blame her. When we arrived on the scene and saw the tail end of the monster, *Magic* and Goliath were having a stand off. *Magic* was puffed up and glowing… Goliath looked like a monster himself… red eyes…huge horns…red, razor sharp, glowing teeth…a sound coming out of him that was hideous beyond belief!" I exclaim.

"Good Heavens! This is really turning into a terror trip…one terror after another…and *Magic* and Goliath or some beastly creature at the center of it. Did anybody else observe these claims of transformations of the dogs?" Dad questions.

"Sarah sees it too!!!!" I exclaim excitedly. "I don't care if you or anybody else believes me. It happens."

Grandma comes walking out of the bedroom drying her hair, "What the heck is going on out here? I must've missed a lot of action last night. I had a very pleasant evening downtown Inverness…while you guys were entrenched in another mystery. I probably should start hanging around with you guys more…if I want some terrifying adventures. I am not so sure I am up for that though."

Dad, and Aunt Rue come and put their arms around my shoulder in an effort to calm me down. "I'm sorry, Paul." Sad says apologetically. "It is just that I would be devastated if anything were to happen to you. I would never forgive myself for bringing you along. That goes for you too Ruthie. I will try to be a little less dramatic, I promise. Just try and keep things down to a low roar instead of this high pitched gear we seem to be heading into," I do have one more question though. Why were you guys all wet?"

Aunt Rue and I look at each other, hesitant to explain. Grandma sits down on the couch and says, "Okay, I want to hear the whole story… from start to finish. Have a seat Noah…we are going to hear what happened last night…"

Inverness is a cool place. There are basketfuls of blue, red, pink, yellow and white flowers hanging along the bridges, outside of houses, stores and just about everywhere. This area of the loch is more like a river, with bridges taking you from one side of the town to the other. The surroundings of such striking contrast…emerald green hills…brilliant colored flowers everywhere…against the slate gray on the buildings, castles and loch, makes the whole place look fantasy like.

As we walk around the town, there are venders selling all kinds of weird wares. One vendor has owls, falcons and other small birds, just sitting on perches. There are food booths, a lot of pubs and there are performers dancing Irish jigs. It is really fun and interesting. It is so curious how different countries have such varying cultures and customs. Surprisingly, my dad lets me go off with all my friends when we meet up. The twins and Adam want to hear about what happened the night before. My dad doesn't say anything warning me. We synchronize our watches and set a time to meet. I guess not much can happen in the middle of Inverness in broad daylight as all the festivities are going on.

Anastasia, Delilah and Adam are disappointed that they missed out on the action of the previous night. Their mom says that they can hang with us tonight. We will be going back to Edinburgh in the morning. I hope everyone will be up for some exploring.

Of course, Adino joins Grandma and Aunt Rue to experience Inverness. I am actually relieved that Adino is hanging around with Aunt Rue and Grandma. He is really nice, has a cool accent and is funny. He also stuck up for us last night. Maybe Aunt Rue and he will keep in touch. She should find someone to share adventures with. He definitely likes adventure. That makes him all right with me.

We all head into the pub and restaurant to get a bite to eat. *Magic* is allowed too. Immediately, after we get settled, we start a plan for the upcoming night. This time we are not going to get into trouble, but we want to explore the castle on Loch Ness at night.

What could happen? *Magic* is always with us.

◆ ◆ ◆ ◆ ◆ ◆

Chapter Twenty-Three
THE TRANSFORMATION

We made a plan in the pub today. Tonight we are going to meet at Adam, Delilah and Anastasia's hotel on Loch Ness at dusk. We are all bringing flashlights, raincoats and umbrellas. Hopefully, it will be a fun time without any more traumatic terrors. One thing I think is weird. Where are Judas and Goliath staying? I didn't see them at our 'Bed and Breakfast', and Jeremiah and Jesse didn't mention seeing them either. I am not sure where the twins and Adam are staying. I am sure that they are at the fancy hotel that looks like a castle down the road from us. It sure is weird how Judas and Goliath were at the same place as us last night. They are always lurking around. Judas' dad seems to be nice enough. I think he was at the pub last night. He was hanging back from the crowd. I did notice him, but I was so distracted from all the action that I forgot to speak with him to see if he saw Judas and Goliath. My dad and the group are all meeting at the pub again.

"So, what are your plans this evening?" Dad asks timidly. "Staying in and playing games with your friends? Doesn't that sound like a safe idea?"

"Well, actually, Delilah, Anastasia and Adam invited us to join them at their hotel. I guess there is a downstairs room where we can gather and have snacks and play games," I reply.

"Oh Good! That sounds like a great idea. We will stop and buy some snacks for you to take. Is it okay to bring *Magic*? You guys should just stay in for the night. I think it might rain," responds dad hopefully.

"Yeah, right. I am sure they will be content to sit around all night playing boring games with a haunted castle and Loch Ness across the street," chides Aunt Rue.

Grandma laughs, "Now don't give those kids any ideas Ruthie. I think I will go along tonight. I don't want to miss out on anything. It will be just my luck that nothing will happen."

"Are you serious? You are looking for action and trying to give Paul ideas? We have had enough terror and mystery for one trip. Let's try and move on with less drama," Dad warns.

"You're no fun, Noah. Since when did you become such an old fuddy-duddy?" Grandma teases. "Besides, you admitted last night that you didn't find anything at the lake except a torn up sheep. It's not like you found total devastation or a monster or anything."

"If we were in America, I would not be so concerned. I would hate to lose my job over indiscretions in a foreign country," replies Dad.

"Oh, don't be so dramatic!" Laughs Grandma. "Rebekah would be surprised at you being so conservative. What happened to the young man who dragged his wife on an African safari, not even caring what danger lurked ahead?"

"I guess I grew up," Dad says. "Besides, Paul and his friends are just kids. You guys make good choices and have fun. That is all I want to say."

"Don't worry dad. What could happen? We always have **Magic** to save the day," I respond.

I hate to sneak around and keep things from my dad and Aunt Rue, but I don't think they would approve of us prowling around again at the lake. Last night was different though. We weren't all together. Tonight there will be more of us. It is always safer when traveling in numbers. What could happen that would be worse than last night?

My dad drops me at the hotel or castle, whatever it is. I am the last to arrive. It is a misty, quietly dubious evening by the lake. The lake is shrouded with a light fog, while the sky seems dark, almost murky with shadows and mottled clouds.

"Is everyone here?" Delilah questions. "I was so angry that our mom did not let us go to the pub last night or get together with all you guys. We missed all the action. I hope we see the monster again tonight."

"I don't know if I am ready for that again," comments Jesse. "It was pretty scary and creepy. The tail was enormous and spiked. It must've reached twenty feet into the air. I would hate to be its next victim. The name 'Nessy' hardly fits the hideous monster we saw."

"Really? I would've screamed… I think," comments Anastasia.

"It all happened so fast, there was no time to scream," replies Sarah. "It was so wild and disturbing. The blood curdling shriek from the monster or black dog was sadistic…and the mutilated sheep was hideously grotesque."

"Wow!" Adam exclaims. "It sounds like I missed all the fun!"

Delilah shoves him, "You would say that."

"Well, it's true. Something terrifying happens, and I miss it," laments Adam.

"All in all, it was horrific. As you said, it was terrifying. The demonic shriek was the worst… Then seeing that sheep… It was disgusting. Thankfully… *Magic* was there. She definitely scared off Goliath," I reply.

"It sounds like I did not get to hear all the details. You will have to fill me in…and…from now on…don't leave me out of these adventures," scolds Adam.

"It was all spur of the moment," Sarah says.

"Well tonight we will be on another adventure. When can we get started?" Adam asks.

"So, let's not stand here talking about adventure, let's go seek some," laughs Jeremiah. "I think all the adults are probably settled in at the pub by now."

"The castle is down the road about a half of a mile," says Anastasia, as we start on our way toward the hill to the path by the loch.

We start out across the street, headed down the slippery, grassy embankment. The grass looks black in the damp, wetness surrounding us. I get a creepy, almost dreadful feeling, and I notice *Magic* is acting weird. She keeps stopping and sniffing around like she senses something. I sense a mysterious sensation engulfing my body. I try and shake it off. I must just be spooked from last night.

"Do you know where Judas and Goliath are staying?" I ask Anastasia.

"Yeah. They are staying in the same hotel we are," replies Anastasia.

"I saw them lurking around on the grounds outside last night," says Delilah.

"Oh, I wondered where they were staying," I reply still trying to act calm and sure of myself.

"Look. Up ahead. Did you see that?" Adam questions.

We all stop in our tracks. We are all a little over cautious after last night. It is not every day you experience a monster...a devil looking dog...a mutilated sheep...not to mention the demonic shriek...all at one time.

"What was it?" I ask hesitantly as my nervous feeling returns.

"Along the path...up there, right before it turns into those bushes. I thought I saw a couple of figures darting around," says Adam.

"Oh no... Shall we turn back?" Sarah questions with a slight whine in her voice. "I honestly am not ready for another show down at the lake."

I hang back to walk with her. "*Magic* is with us...don't worry. I won't let anything happen to you. All of you girls*...* Drop back and walk with Sarah and *Magic*. We boys will be in front. *Magic* will guard you girls...right *Magic?*" I say as I look at *Magic*, trying to sound positive, and pet her head. Immediately, *Magic* drops back...just as if she heard and understood every word I said. I can tell she is on high alert.

"She is so cute," says Delilah. "I feel safer with her hanging with us."

"If you guys want to turn back, we can," I say almost wishing we hadn't come.

"No, that's okay. We have *Magic*," They reply.

"Up ahead. Did you see that? It is like a cloaked figure and something smaller, like an animal," whispers Jesse.

"Let's go catch them," whispers Adam.

"Don't leave us by ourselves," The girls plead.

We charge ahead through the massive bushes and around the bend. There is nothing.

"You must've been seeing things," says Jeremiah.

"Let's wait for the girls." I say. "Here they are. Hey, it was nothing. Let's head to the castle. I really want to explore the ruins before something prevents us from doing that."

"You lead the way," says Adam.

The ruins are amazing. They date back to the thirteenth century. It is hard to believe these stairs have been here that long. Suddenly the moon clears the clouds and brightens our way; we don't need to use our flashlights much. It stops misting too. It is becoming an awesome night.

We are all pretty quiet while we investigate the nooks and crannies of the ruins. Maybe it was the dark, shadowy clouds that were so haunting. I am starting to feel more confident as we explore the ruins.

It is amazing to think of all the battles that were fought here and all the soldiers who lived here. I love this land. Scotland is the coolest place ever, even if it is a little spooky sometimes. I am so glad that we came out tonight. I don't think anything could ruin the experience now. I don't know why I felt so weird before, but it is turning into an awesome night. I felt relief.

"Wow! This is amazing!... This is awesome!... This is old and remarkable... I am so glad we are exploring this at night!... Check out the moon!... What an awesome night!!!" Everyone comments.

We all stand quietly enjoying God's splendor, for that is what it is. The sky and stars that have been suddenly revealed are truly an amazing miracle.

A hideous, demonic shriek breaks the silence.

"Oh my gosh!!! There is that awful shriek again!" Sarah screams.

"Let's go!" I yell as I take off running with **Magic** sprinting ahead.

Everyone follows. No one wants to be left behind by themselves. Suddenly the serene, mellow atmosphere turns to a chilling, unnerving gloom. The shriek heightens and soars to new guttural, frantic cries. I hear voices coming from all directions.

Who's here? I can't imagine who is out here. **Magic** disappears behind a bend and disappears into a clump of trees. The lake looks like it's in turmoil. It almost looks like a boat was winding along the shore. Maybe that is what it is. A boat. I scurry around the curve and come out on a clearing. Oh no!! What is that?!!!!

On the shore is a black creature's neck and head rearing about twenty feet out of the lake. The neck is long and skinny and the head is like a crocodile's with the biggest mouth and teeth I have ever seen!

I hear the girl's screaming hysterically, warning **Magic.** I see **Magic** running toward the monsters mouth...its body is partially submerged...

the tail is breaking through the water…careening back and forth in the air about twenty feet high! I stop… There stand Judas and Goliath… *Magic* transforms into her puffed up glowing glory…while Goliath is lunging at the monster…his glistening, crimson teeth…his massive horns…red glowing eyes! The monster's jaws snap shut and Goliath jumps out of the way! Oh no… *Magic* is trying to put herself between the monster and Goliath!

I scream, "NOOOOOOO *MAGIC*!!!!!!!!!!!!!!! NOOOOOOOOO OOOOO."

I race forward. Suddenly this hand grabs me back. It is my dad. I start fighting him. "Let me go, let me go… I have got to help her." My dad wraps his arms around me along with Adino as I try to struggle free. I start crying and screaming "*Magic, Magic!*"

"NO, PAUL, NO PAUL," Aunt Rue is screaming at the top of her lungs as she races towards us in all the confusion.

The girls are all holding each other as the others stand with their mouths gaping at the scene.

The slimy, purplish monster lunges again…as *Magic* jumps between it and Goliath. The monster rolls over to snatch *Magic*…she punches it under the jaw with her engorged back legs…just as it snaps it mouth shut and catches Goliath's back leg. *Magic* bites the monster's neck. With a blood curdling squeal…an explosion of blood…the monster's tail slaps the water, sending an enormous wave engulfing everyone standing around. It slinks back under the water…leaving in its wake a bloody, foamy aftermath. *Magic* is flung aside on the shore.

There on the foamy shore lay Goliath and Judas, a bloody mess. Judas had slipped and whacked his head on a rock. Judas' dad goes running, grabbing Judas head up in his arms…cradling him.

My dad, Adino and Aunt Rue still hold me. *Magic*, gets up covered in blood, still glowing and slightly engorged, head drooping and walks to Goliath and Judas. She climbs on Judas and licks his head…where it is wounded, his dad still cradling him. She starts to glow brighter and lays her head on his chest. He moves slightly…but still is lifeless. Everyone is silent.

Magic gets off of Judas and limps to Goliath. She covers him with her glowing, puffy body…starts to lick his face and his wounds. His tail moves and ***Magic*** eases off of him. She lies on her stomach and puts her head down on her paws…whines and fades back to normal color and size.

As Judas and Goliath lay on the silent shore, there is a trembling of the ground that causes everyone to grip each other. Immediately, a swishing, sucking, deafening sound emerges from the air and Judas and Goliaths' bodies become stiff as boards. A gray mist rises out of their bodies and disappears into the air. It is eerily silent and calm. Suddenly, Judas sits upright and looks around himself…sees his dad and embraces him. Goliath sits up, barks and starts licking ***Magic.***

Judas exclaims and questions, "What happened. Why am I all wet… who are all these people? Where are we? Is Goliath okay?"

My dad releases me and I run to ***Magic,*** still bloody and matted looking. She starts jumping around with Goliath as they play.

Instantly…the earth rumbles with thunder…lightening strikes the water, illuminating it …the sky opens and pours freezing, gigantic rain drops on everything. Everyone stands in awe of what just happened.

After what seems an eternity, Adino finally gathers everyone up and herds us back to the pub, Judas and Goliath included.

I turn to call ***Magic*** and there she is…standing by the shore… washed clean…looking at me… ***Glowing***…just for me.

◆ ◆ ◆ ◆ ◆ ◆

Chapter Twenty-Four
CELEBRATION OF LIFE

The pub is in an uproar with all that has happened. The pouring rain is just another added excitement, as it always is. There is something about rain pouring from the sky that stirs everything up. *Magic* is the guest of honor, as she should be. Everyone is talking about what happened. Actually, Judas and Goliath are also being lauded and receiving accolades of praise. They are as miraculous as *Magic.*

I don't think anyone will ever doubt again that *Magic* is special.

Judas and I shake hands and Goliath licks me and wags his tail at everyone. Judas' dad is so happy and jovial. He buys everyone a drink that is in the pub. We kids get crème soda, which is delicious. We even give the dogs some.

We sit at the table near the fireplace trying to get dry and warm and talk about what happened. No one knows what to think. Everyone has a theory about what we all witnessed. Some think that the monster has something to do with the transformation of Judas and Goliath.

"I think it is divine intervention," Jesse says. "My dad is always telling me that God is watching over us, especially teenagers. I just thought he was kidding…you know…teasing me about my adventures…but… now…I am pretty sure my dad is right. I don't know about you guys, but it was an awesome experience that only God could have orchestrated. The devil and God definitely had a battle tonight!"

"*Magic* is key in all of this," Sarah adds. "I think she must be a guardian angel watching out for us. I love her and how she is so unbelievably brilliant!!!"

"Here, Here," salutes Adam as he raises his glass in a toast.

We all raise our glasses and toast ***Magic***. She sits on her tail and rises up like she is dancing.

Anastasia adds, "I never knew that the devil really existed. Now that I have seen what can happen when the devil is involved, I will definitely be staying positive and faithful to God. I think it must be the positive bond we all had together that gave ***Magic*** the strength to perform like she did."

"All I know is that all of you, including the dogs, are amazing. I don't think that I have ever felt so close to any other friends. You're right Jesse. I believe this was a God thing." Sarah announces.

Everyone raises their glasses and says, "Amen!"

♦ ♦ ♦ ♦ ♦ ♦ ♦

Chapter Twenty-Five
RESOLUTION

It was a hard night for everyone. No one seemed to be able to sleep through the night. We are anxious to get back on the road to go back to Edinburgh, as a last minute change in itinerary. I loved Edinburgh and am excited about going back. I don't think I ever missed my mom more than I do right now. She always could make sense of everything, and, if she couldn't, she had a knack of focusing on the positive. I know my dad must miss her at times like this. She could explain stuff really well. *Magic* is lying next to me like nothing ever happened. I wish she could talk, for I know she would be comforting as well. "Come on *Magic*, let's go find Dad."

"You're up. I had a rough night. I think we all did. I kept running into everyone all night up for one thing or another," I say to Dad.

"Yeah, it was one of those nights." Dad says with a laugh. "Come sit next to me... I love you son. I am so glad I brought you and *Magic* on this trip. Yeah... *Magic.* I learned a lot from you two this vacation. I need to pay more attention to you and what you think and less attention to my conventions. Aunt Rue and you are usually right-on with what you are sensing and experiencing, and I need to be more aware of that. You know, sometimes, when a person gets older and has lots of responsibilities, the most important signs of miraculous things are overlooked. I need to slow down a bit and get back some of my old perspective, like you have and your Aunt Rue still have."

"What happened at the lake last night, Dad? What was that all about, and why are Judas and Goliath acting like...like a regular guy and dog now?" I ask.

"Paul, there is good and evil in the world," Dad says. "God is good and the Devil is evil. The word *devil* in English contains the word evil. Satan is another name for the evil in the world. When a person is weak in the Lord or a non-believer, Satan sneaks in. If people don't have God in their life, they are very vulnerable to all kinds of influences, especially evil ones. Satan loves a weak believer or non-believer. He wants to turn everyone against the Lord. He was kicked out of Heaven, and he never got over it. He even tried to tempt Jesus in the desert, remember? Jesus was wandering for forty days and Satan tried to tempt him the whole time, but Jesus was too committed to even consider what Satan was offering. Sometimes Satan will enter into someone and take over his or her body. The Bible says that, when Jesus was performing all his miracles, he would call the Devil out of people who were behaving badly. Miraculously, the suffering person would be cured because Jesus was able to run the evil spirit out."

"Yeah, I know those accounts. So...do you think that was what was wrong with Judas and Goliath? Was Satan in them? Is that what we saw leave their bodies? ...That gray stuff? Judas was confused, like he didn't remember anything. It was so scary, Dad. I thought **Magic** was going to die trying to save Goliath. Why did she do that? What was that all about?" I question.

"Paul, I can only guess what happened. God is in charge, like I always tell you. God has a plan for us, and sometimes it is unclear what he is up to. I wish your mom were here in times like this. She had such insight into the ways of life. If I have to make sense of this, I think that you are right. Satan had taken up residence in Judas and Goliath for the past few years. It seems his influence became worse and worse on the boy over the years. His dad has been pretty quiet on this trip. I wondered if he was worried about his boy. Maybe he brought his son and dog on this trip to keep an eye on them. That is why I tried to be positive and discourage you from judging him. I see now that I was foolish in not being as alert to danger as you and your Aunt Rue. I know now that you are right about **Magic**. There is something very special about her, even though I do not see what you see. I must apologize about making fun of you and your claims. Maybe someday I will experience what you have with Magic. No dog could have done what **Magic** did, even a vicious dog...well...like Goliath. It was miraculous to watch her in action. I did see that gray cloud leave Judas' and Goliath's bodies. It was miraculous and, as you say, scary. What did you see, Paul?" Dad asks.

"You're not going to laugh? Promise?" I respond.

"I promise." Dad reassures me.

"Well, like I said before. **Magic** puffed up about three times her size," I begin. "She became a massive fur ball and started glowing in a neon yellow, like lightening, her eyes were glowing the same way. She became strong and ferocious and invincible. The Loch Ness monster and Goliath was no match for **Magic**. Goliath had huge razor sharp horns, about a foot long,...fiery, orange-red eyes ...glowing, crimson teeth and was also puffed up about three times his size!" I describe incredulously.

"I am almost glad I didn't see all that. You are a brave boy!!" Dad exclaims.

"Sarah saw it too. I mentioned that to you yesterday. She told me at the Tattoo performance that she felt **Magic** get really warm, start to glow and puff up before he lunged under the bleachers. She saw what I saw last night too. We shared with each other before we left the pub last night. No one else heard though. I don't think it matters anyway because everyone knows **Magic** is special now, whether they saw her transform or not," I reply. "Sarah agrees."

"What? You mean there was an incident at the Tattoo performance too?" Dad questions.

"Are you kidding? That is only one of many I have seen or attempted to tell you about," I reply laughing.

"Well, it appears that **Magic** literally scared the devil out of Judas and Goliath. I wonder if the monster will recover from the wrath of **Magic**? You know... Sarah must be as special as you." Dad ponders.

"I have never met anyone who could see **Magic's** tricks except Sarah. Her mom died too, when she was giving birth to her baby brother. He died too." I say.

"Well...that is food for thought and very sad for her and her dad." Replies Dad.

"All I know is that we have to take ***Magic*** on all our trips. Right, Dad?" I respond.

"I think we have our own personal angel on board. I will never take another trip without my family. As a matter of fact, our director mentioned that she was thinking of signing a contract for a European filming adventure," Dad offers.

Dad calls ***Magic*** over and hugs her. "No, I don't think we will ever go on another adventure without our ***Magic.***"

"She is ***OUR Magic.***"

♦♦♦♦♦♦

ACKNOWLEDGEMENTS

I would like to thank all of those who made it possible for me to finish my first novel. Somehow, over the course of the writing of this novel, many people became involved. I have often wondered how so many people can become involved in the creation of a publication. I now know how that happens. It happens because people care about each other. I never dreamed that so many people would come forth to help me.

My children and our adventures while traveling provided inspiration for my story. Paul, my son, is the inspiration for the main character. Michelle, my daughter, is the illustrator. Michelle is such a busy person, but she took time to do the illustrations for me. I cannot thank her enough, especially for the dog sketch. I love photography, so on my travels I am always photographing everything of interest to use in my books. I do not want to forget to mention our beautiful golden retriever, Wiley. He was truly a magical dog for all of us.

All ages contributed to my success at publishing this novel. I have to say that my former students at Southwestern Christian School and Victory Christian Academy in Chula Vista, San Diego were the ones who encouraged me with enthusiasm from the very beginning of the project. They were constantly pushing me to finish. It is hard to stay focused on a large project that is so massively time consuming, so I would take breaks from creating my story. My students were relentless and fascinated with the whole idea. They were truly inspiring as my students.

Some of my friends encouraged me to actualize this dream of being an author of teenage books, which I adore reading and writing. Several of my friends read my manuscript and gave feedback about the story and its accuracy. One friend in particular, Anne Jones, read the story and helped me with the editing. Bob Giffin also helped with editing. What awesome friends!!

www.ingramcontent.com/pod-product-compliance
Lightning Source LLC
Chambersburg PA
CBHW050456110726
47899CB00003B/964